WESSEX

King Midas, Mompesson House

Glastonbury Tor

A NATIONAL TRUST BOOK

WESSEX

Text by Patricia Beer

Photographs by Fay Godwin

HAMISH HAMILTON
LONDON

Books by Patricia Beer

Poetry
Loss of the Magyar
The Survivors
Just Like the Resurrection
The Estuary
Driving West
Selected Poems
The Lie of the Land

Autobiography
Mrs Beer's House

Novel
Moon's Ottery

Criticism
Reader, I Married Him

Books by Fay Godwin

The Oldest Road, An Exploration of the Ridgeway, with J R L Anderson
The Oil Rush with Mervyn Jones
The Drovers Roads of Wales with Shirley Toulson
Islands with John Fowles
Remains of Elmet with Ted Hughes
Romney Marsh with Richard Ingrams
Tess, The Story of a Guide Dog with Peter Purves
The Whisky Roads of Scotland with Derek Cooper
Bison at Chalk Farm
The Saxon Shore Way with Alan Sillitoe
Land, with an essay by John Fowles

First published in Great Britain 1985
by Hamish Hamilton Ltd.
Garden House 57–59 Long Acre London WC2E 9JZ

Permission has kindly been given by Faber & Faber Ltd., to reprint lines from 'Wessex Guide Book' taken from *The Collected Poems of Louis MacNeice* and from 'Generation' taken from *Collected Poems 1909–1962* by T S Eliot.

Book design by Norman Reynolds

Map drawn by Patrick Leeson

British Library Cataloguing in Publication Data

Beer, Patricia
   Wessex: a National Trust book.
   1. Wessex (England)—Description and travel
   —Guide-books
   I. Title   II. Godwin, Fay
   914.23   DA670.W48

   ISBN 0-241-11550-7

Typeset by Rowland Phototypesetting Ltd.,
Bury St Edmunds, Suffolk
Printed and bound in Italy
by Arnoldo Mondadori Editore, Verona

The photographs are for Tony Stokes

I wish to thank the many officials of the National Trust who have helped me in my writing of *Wessex*, and particularly Tom Burr, John Carslake and Geoffrey Hordley, Head Forester on the Holnicote Estate, whose deep and affectionate knowledge of the trees in his charge made a walk through Horner and Selworthy Woods a memorable experience.

I have acknowledged in the text many books which have enlightened me on various aspects of Wessex, but I must single out Anne Acland's *A Devon Family*, an account of the Acland family, Devon landowners for 800 years, who also owned the Holnicote Estate in Somerset, one of the earliest and still one of the most important gifts to the National Trust. Lady Acland's fascinating information, being based on family records, would have been obtainable in no easy way except through her book.

Finally I thank my husband, Damien Parsons, to whom the text is dedicated. He accompanied me on nearly all my expeditions; his knowledge, his comments, and his enthusiasm for the project were unfailingly supportive to me.

Patricia Beer

I am grateful for an enormous amount of help while working on *Wessex*, from far too many people to name, but would like to thank especially: Jenny and Brian Doyle, Rosemary Goad, Valerie Lloyd, and Shirley Toulson for their help and hospitality; Robert Lassam, Curator of Fox Talbot Museum for his encouragement which cheered me on more than I can say; and finally very special thanks to Peter Cattrell for printing the photographs.

Fay Godwin

Corfe Castle, from the south

CONTENTS

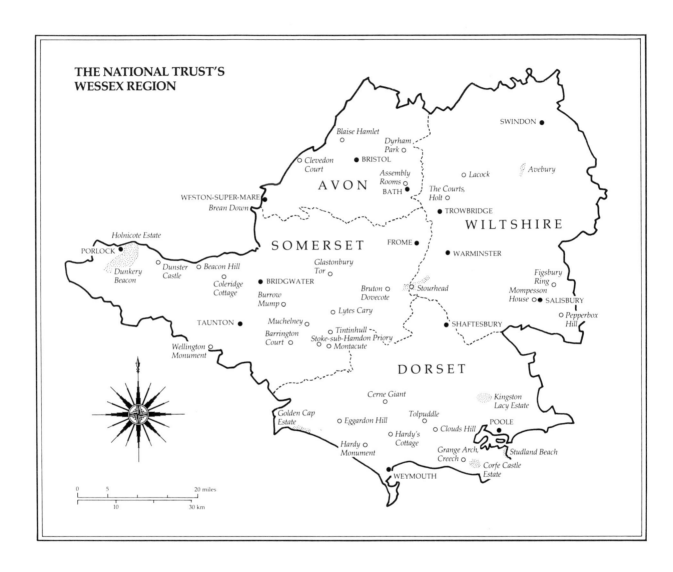

THE NATIONAL TRUST'S
WESSEX REGION

SWINDON

Blaise Hamlet
Dyrham
Park
Clevedon
Court
BRISTOL
Avebury
Lacock

AVON
Assembly
Rooms
BATH
The Courts,
Holt
WESTON-SUPER-MARE
Brean Down
TROWBRIDGE
WILTSHIRE

SOMERSET
FROME

Holnicote Estate
PORLOCK
WARMINSTER
Glastonbury
Tor
Figsbury
Ring
Dunkery
Beacon
Dunster
Castle
Beacon Hill
Coleridge
Cottage
BRIDGWATER
Bruton
Dovecote
Stourhead
Mompesson
House
SALISBURY
Burrow
Mump
Lytes Cary
SHAFTESBURY
Pepperbox
Hill
TAUNTON
Muchelney
Barrington
Court
Tintinhull
Stoke-sub-Hamdon Priory
Montacute
Wellington
Monument

DORSET

Cerne Giant
Kingston
Lacy Estate
Golden Cap
Estate
Eggardon Hill
Tolpuddle
Clouds Hill
POOLE
Hardy's
Cottage
Studland Beach
Hardy
Monument
Grange Arch,
Creech
Corfe Castle
Estate
WEYMOUTH

0   5   20 miles
   10   30 km

INTRODUCTION

Ever since the coming of the Saxons the name Wessex has been variously bestowed; perhaps most oddly of all on Thomas Hardy's evil-tempered dog, but even in the case of territory always idiosyncratically. The Wessex of this book is that of the National Trust. For sound administrative reasons the Trust's kingdom goes less far east than King Alfred's Wessex, in excluding Hampshire, and less far west than Hardy's, in excluding Devon and incidentally myself. It consists of four counties, three of them ancient, one an upstart: Wiltshire, Somerset, Dorset and Avon.

There is a further contraction: not only is the terrain limited in this way but no properties are described in any detail except those managed by the Trust; so no Longleat and no Forde Abbey, no Creech Grange only the Arch, no Stonehenge only the Down. But a list of what the Trust does own in Wessex will, I think, leave nobody feeling deprived, for it includes Kingston Lacy House, Corfe Castle (and indeed the whole of the recently-acquired Bankes Estate), Montacute, Stourhead, Dyrham Park, and the splendid estates of Holnicote and Golden Cap.

The wealth of the material needs no further comment but its disparity does, in so far as it demands a particular technique. An account of Wessex that was of its nature chronological, historical or geographical would have to be comprehensive to make much sense. In this present discussion of the region, selectivity is inherent in the subject matter, so none of these techniques would do, except in snatches. Indeed they might blur the details.

A thematic approach seemed to be the answer, so the text consists of fourteen essays, each of which is more or less self-contained, though naturally there is a great deal of cross-reference. And as the work took shape it occurred to me that this method was sharpening rather than blurring much of the material. The motives of all those rich men (Andrew Napper, Peter Lyte, Henry Hoare I) who throughout the centuries 'pulled down their barns and built greater' must always have been much the same but the results were significantly various. The poor men who lived in houses that were undeniably poky (though Coleridge went too far in calling his cottage at Nether Stowey a 'lowly shed') do gain from being thought of together. So do eye-catchers, whether they were built to keep doves in, honour a hero, form a view, watch the hunt from, or simply to spite the neighbours.

Of course the danger of the thematic approach is that it is a net through which things could slip. I hope readers looking for a subject that interests them particularly will not find that it has got away.

Patricia Beer

Chapter 1

ABBEY AND CASTLE

FOR CENTURIES now people not professionally religious have been living in abbeys and people with no expectation of being physically attacked have been living in castles. What they have made of the buildings they bought or stole varies greatly of course; and opinion as to when it becomes ridiculous to go on calling a house an abbey or a castle also varies.

There is disagreement too about what really was an abbey or a castle in the first place. Writers about either have often been so highly selective as to leave themselves with a very short shortlist. Victoria Sackville-West in her *English Country Houses* (1941) is very selective indeed, especially about castles. She dismisses out of hand all those so-called castles that 'were never intended to withstand an attacking force but carried on the tradition of feudalism long after the necessity for defence had disappeared'. She becomes quite waspish in her purism: 'There was Stokesay in Salop, where Sir Lawrence of Ludlow went to the quite unnecessary trouble of obtaining the royal licence to crenellate.'

Henry James is much more lenient. In the essay 'Abbeys and Castles' which he wrote in 1877 he by no means rules out the so-called castles. He admits they are phoney and in fact singles out Stokesay Castle as an example, but instead of lambasting it and its maker he seems to think all the better of them. Stokesay 'must have assumed its present shape at a time when people had ceased to peer through narrow slits at possible besiegers. There are slits in the outer walls for such peering, but they are noticeably broad and not particularly oblique, and might easily have been applied to the uses of a peaceful parley.' But for James 'this is part of the charm of the place; human life there must have lost an earlier grimness;

it was lived in by people who were beginning to believe in good intentions.'

Dunster Castle in Somerset might possibly have satisfied Victoria Sackville-West as to date. There was a fortification, a sort of tower, on the site in Saxon times; the earliest building that might properly be called a castle was erected by William de Mohun who came over with William the Conqueror. And it was not some fortified manor house romantically posing as a castle; as late as the Civil War it was fighting for its life and that of the Royalist cause. Not that the Luttrells, who had acquired it in the fourteenth century, were Royalists. They had active Parliamentarian sympathies and relatives, and indeed at one point Mrs Thomas Luttrell personally opened fire on the Royalists from the castle; but, with the mounting successes of King Charles's supporters in the south-west in 1643, Thomas Luttrell thought it prudent to surrender to the apparent victors, and Francis Wyndham was made Governor of the castle. In the following year, of course, the tide of battle turned and the castle was implacably besieged for a hundred and sixty days by the Parliamentarians. Wyndham fought well but at last in his turn surrendered.

But if Dunster fulfilled two of Sackville-West's criteria it must have failed on the point of extensive rebuilding. So much has been pulled down, so much put up, that it really is difficult to imagine what Dunster must once have been like. One can get some cerebral notion of it from a close study of books and maps, but such studies do tend to stultify the imagination. The imagination of most people, that is to say; Henry James had no trouble at all. In his reflections on Stokesay he cheats with dash and ingenuity. Faithfully following his own advice ('Dramatise') he brings life back: the people stepping out of the chamber at the top of the staircase

whose rugged wooden logs, by way of steps, and solid, deeply guttered hand-rail, still remain. They looked down into the hall where, I take it, there was always a congregation of retainers, much lounging and waiting and passing to and fro, with a door open into the court. The court, as I said just now, was not the grassy aesthetic spot which you may find it at present of a summer's day; there were beasts tethered in it, and hustling men at arms, and the earth was trampled into puddles. But my lord or my lady, looking down from the chamber-door, commanded the position and, no doubt, issued their orders accordingly.

This is shamelessly padded – logs usually are wooden – but it is

Dunster Castle

Cellarage, Dunster Castle

constructive. The real weakness of the technique is that it makes everything – in this case castles – sound exactly the same. Surely it is more interesting to note, in each example, what exactly can be observed, however vestigially, of a former existence.

There is nothing vestigial about the site of Dunster Castle. It is still, as it must always have been, a complete and natural stronghold. The tor stands alone, near the Quantocks and the Brendons and Exmoor but essentially independent of them all. The River Avill runs by on the east side and in the middle ages was navigable right up to the foot of the tor; indeed there was a port there. These are the practical assets. Psychologically, the castle must have looked impregnable, and indeed a hundred and sixty days against Fairfax's troops was an impressive enough stand, and led to plans of poisoning the water supply and other acts of desperate malpractice on the part of the attackers. It still looks formidable as well as picturesque, especially as one comes round the corner on the A39 from the east: every inch a castle.

Pevsner says of Dunster that 'archaeologically it has not much to offer – two gatehouses and some masonry'. This disobliging comment is true to Pevsner's character but not to the facts as most people would interpret them. Certainly nothing remains of the Saxon fortification and very little of the medieval castle, but such traces as there are need no Jamesian theatricals to make them truly exciting.

The Stables, Dunster Castle

The castle passed into the possession of the Luttrell family, by what can only be described as a series of fiddles, at the beginning of the fifteenth century. It was not the Luttrells who fiddled but Lady Joan de Mohun, who before she could sell her husband's castle to anybody had to get it into her own hands first. She then sold it to Lady Elizabeth Luttrell for a handsome sum on condition that she was given tenure for life. The deal was concluded and she received the money. She then lived on for thirty years, but of course this was not a fiddle, more a praiseworthy human instinct. Incidentally there must always have been something about Dunster Castle that fostered the matriarchal spirit. It can be no coincidence that both the Mohun family and the Luttrell family included so many strong-minded and resourceful women.

Vestiges, whatever Pevsner says, are the way to enjoy almost anything older than yesterday. As you pant up to Dunster Castle and reach the first gatehouse, built by Sir Hugh Luttrell in 1420, you notice that the windows, of almost drawing-room width and decorated with pretty tracery, do not seem quite right for a fortification. Then you notice the arches rising just above them, narrower and more austere, the remains of windows at least a century older, that really were part of a defensive design. And as you then turn right, through a gateway built by a Mohun, and start up a flight of nineteenth-century steps you see below you to the left a cobbled path rising much more gradually than the steps but clearly bound for the outer ward as well.

The Green Court, as the outer ward is now called, is aptly named. The Luttrells gave considerable time and thought to the greening of their castle. In the fifteenth century as the sea drew back they planted the lower slopes of the tor. When the Green Court was formed in the eighteenth century, by the levelling of the slope up to the keep, they grassed it right across, as we know from contemporary watercolours, with only a small path round it. (Today a drive cuts centrally through it.) Perhaps the most revolutionary act of all was when they formed a bowling green on the site of the keep. It provokes one to an Omar Khayyam/Fitzgerald type of meditation:

> Think how the Warriors lie buried deep
> Yet Mohun after Mohun stirs in Sleep
> Dreaming of distant Drums, to hear the Tramp
> Of Luttrells playing Bowls upon the Keep.

In spite of time and change it is easy to see the layout of the castle. The house is a different matter. In 1617 George Luttrell commissioned William Arnold to build a new house on the site of earlier living quarters. It was rather on the principle of a Russian doll, an entity within the separate entity of the fortifications. This was to stand the Luttrells in good stead, for when, after the execution of Charles I and three years after Wyndham's surrender, the Parliamentarian forces returned to demolish it as a fortress in case of future trouble, at least they were able to do so without materially harming the dwelling.

No further wars threatened the house. It was a close-run thing, though, at the time of the Monmouth rebellion, but the Francis Luttrell of the day must have been a clever man if not an out-and-out trimmer, for nobody has ever been sure which side he was on, and in the south-west it would have been very difficult to be neutral. My favourite story – a cheerful one out of such distress – is how

The South Terrace, Dunster
Castle

Mill stream, Dunster Castle Mill

Colonel Luttrell set out with the men of Dunster in support of *Monmouth*. Mysteriously it took them a week to get to Sedgemoor and by then the battle had just been lost by their hero. The Colonel got his followers back to Dunster in two hours – it must have been at the double – and by the time law and order arrived, eager for reprisals, the men were working away in the fields, all affable surprise at the news.

Inside the house it is not so much vestiges as time capsules. It is like science fiction to go through the Outer and Inner Hall, remodelled in Victorian times by Anthony Salvin for George Fownes Luttrell, walk up the oak staircase installed by Francis Luttrell in the 1680s, and enter the morning room created by Henry Fownes Luttrell in the late eighteenth century: disconcerting but suggestive. There is much pleasure to be got from the work of every age: individual items like the brass gasolier in the drawing room, or whole rooms like Salvin's charming library which is inviting to the point of temptation.

There is much that is restless. In and out of the turbulent wooden foliage of Francis Luttrell's gorgeous staircase, every animate thing, cherubic or four-legged, chases something else upstairs. On the same lines, the dining room has the most exhausting ceiling I have ever tried to contemplate.

None of this has anything to do with Dunster's being a castle. For a long time now the interior has been thoroughly domestic, from priest-hole to breakfast-room. Its surroundings too have long since borne tokens of peaceful civilisation: the summerhouse at the side of the keep, the terrace with its flower beds and giant lemon tree, the mimosa on the slopes, and at the foot of the tor the pasture land and the working mill, the deer park and in the twentieth century the polo ground.

It is only the outside that has a claim still to be called a castle. That claim is strong, however, thanks to Salvin who as a good Victorian knew what a castle ought to look like. He respected its earlier appearance but felt it his duty to improve on it, enlarging and rearranging towers and adding a prominent picture-book turret. Even a Martian would realise it was a castle, especially in the morning light. Humphry Repton's dictum, that whereas landscape gains from having the light behind it buildings look best with the light full on them, is amply borne out by Dunster Castle. In the evening it can look quite tame.

Jane Austen, one cannot help feeling, was essentially un-

Winnowing machine, still in working order, Dunster Castle Mill

19

impressed by castles and abbeys. The whole-hearted way she uses them for the laughs goes rather beyond what characterization and plot require. Catherine Morland's abortive expedition to Blaise Castle is not so much comedy as farce – especially if one knows, as presumably Jane Austen did, that it was a folly, not at all 'like what one reads of' – and the collapse of her expectations of Northanger Abbey is a joke that goes on too long, apparently for its own sake.

Northanger is not Jane Austen's only abbey. Mr Knightley lives in one too, but in this case its origins are not worth even a giggle; they are completely ignored. We assume the absence of cloisters and stoups as we accept the presence of every modern comfort. We get no picture of Donwell Abbey beyond Emma's reflection, at the strawberry-gathering party, that it was obviously the residence of a family of true gentility, a house that could not raise a blush in any of Mr Knightley's connections, not even herself.

Both Catherine Morland and Emma Woodhouse would have found what they wanted in Lacock Abbey, Wiltshire. It would have been genteel enough for Emma and romantic enough for Catherine. The first sight of it does not correspond in every detail to Catherine's expectations on the way to Northanger:

> Every bend in the road was expected with solemn awe to afford a glimpse of its massy walls of grey stone, rising amidst a grove of ancient oaks, with the last beams of the sun playing in beautiful splendour on its high Gothic windows;

Gothick arch and clock tower, Lacock Abbey

but though, in its quiet water meadows with the River Avon slipping by, it looks more serene than any building erected on the wilder shores of Catherine's imagination, it has great dignity and presence.

Henry James loved converted abbeys and stayed in them as often as he was invited. Fortunately there were a great many: 'You get an impression that when Catholic England was in her prime great abbeys were as thick as milestones.' He enjoyed the intrusion of what he calls 'the tokens of the remote' on his own everyday living: 'To see one of the small monkish masks grinning at you while you dress and undress, or while you look up in the intervals of inspiration from your letter-writing, is a mere detail in the entertainment of living in a *ci-devant* priory.'

The average visitor, in the more usual sense of day-tripper, to a converted abbey in our times does not normally dress and undress while there or catch up with his correspondence, but plods on round the building, holding one of the informative ping-pong bats provided. Yet he 'inhales the historic' as well as James did, and it often takes exactly the same form. Certainly it does at Lacock. Two medieval carvings which once supported the roof beams of the refectory peer into the Brown Gallery just as their counterparts did into James's bedroom. 'The flags worn away by monkish sandals', which he noticed (or said he did; if no footprints had existed he would have invented them), are here too, just off the Brown Gallery. There were nuns inside the sandals not monks, and the flags they wore down are isolated from us by a sheet of glass, but we can 'devour the documentary' – another phrase of James's – nevertheless.

The nuns were Augustinian canonesses, well-born wealthy women. There were usually about twenty of them and various lay sisters to do the rough. Their abbey was founded in 1232 by Ela, a remarkable woman of remarkable family – the Earls of Salisbury – married to an even more remarkable man: William Longespee, illegitimate son of Henry II, powerful baron, witness of Magna Carta and co-founder of Salisbury Cathedral, where he is buried.

If you want a monument to Ela look at the ground floor of the abbey, that still exists today under the first-floor dwelling: the cloister court, the chapter house, the warming room and all the remains of an ordered holy everyday life. That is her most evocative and authentic memorial, but the tributes to her that adorn the present hall show considerable spirit. The hall was built in 1754–5 – at the command of John Ivory Talbot, owner at the time – by Sanderson Miller in the Gothick style that was his speciality. To provide occupants for Sanderson Miller's Gothick niches Talbot commissioned Victor Alexander Sederbach, a fashionable Austrian sculptor, who produced a series of gesticulating terracotta figures in every attitude of defiance, submission, exhortation, rapture and theatrical absent-mindedness. They are said to be Ela and close members of her family, and look quite lively enough to be so.

In his pursuit of abbeys as well as of castles Henry James was a great believer in the eye of fancy, which 'might see the ghosts of monks and the shadows of abbots pass noiselessly to and fro'. With respect, this is too easy, too like Catherine Morland who possessed not only the eye of fancy but its ear too: she had expected the Northanger breeze to waft the sighs of the murdered to her.

(Overleaf, left)
North cloister, Lacock Abbey

(Overleaf, right)
Cloister vaulting, Lacock Abbey

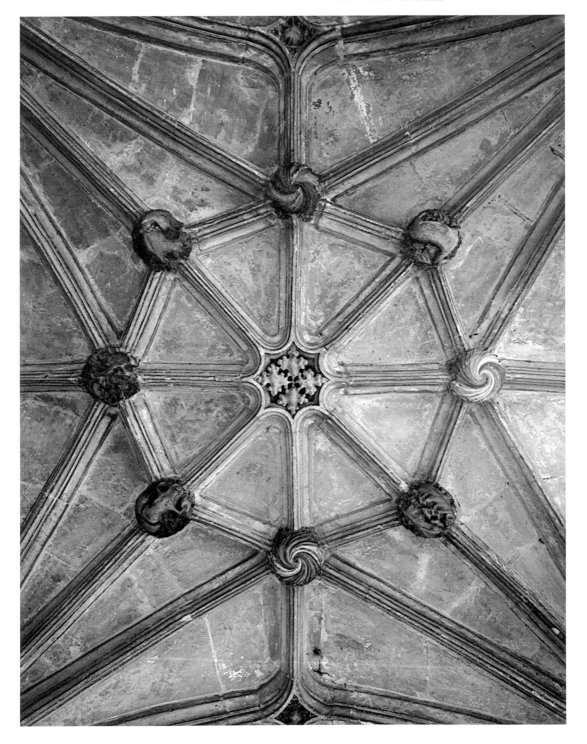

In any case at Lacock a very fanciful eye is not necessary. From the elegant eighteenth-century dining room on the first floor a spiral staircase leads down to the cloisters from what was once the abbess's private apartment, and any visitor not pathologically short of imagination could hear the hem of a nun's habit softly thudding down the steps, or in the cloisters see sick nuns being bundled along the passage to the infirmary.

However, at Lacock I feel it is best to dispense with fancy altogether. Observation is much more rewarding. The south front of the abbey, particularly, repays concentration of the most precise and least fanciful kind. It is a vertical palimpsest. It was originally the north wall of the abbey church, which was destroyed at the time of the dissolution of the monasteries when the new owner William Sharington converted the abbey buildings into a private house.

Sharington was no vandal, and was responsible for better actions than this, such as the preservation of so large a part of the original nunnery. Yet he was no mere preservationist. The handsome octagonal tower he built at the south-east corner of the new secularised mansion adds greatly to its beauty.

The vanished church has left indelible marks on the wall which suddenly became the outside of a house. Moving westward along the south front we can see the extent of the church. Sharington's tower is where its north-east corner must have been; a buttress near the other end of the façade marks its north-west corner. It is between these two points that the present interest lies. Three large nineteenth-century oriel windows jut out into what would have been the medieval church. (One of them, because of the connection with William Henry Fox Talbot, is much the best known.) There are also signs that an earlier life moved in the opposite direction; the church jutted into the dwelling. One doorway, now next to Sharington's tower, led from the church to the sacristy in the main building; there are vestiges of another through which the nuns returned to their dormitory. There are traces of arches and a hole where the rood beam rested.

In any discussion of converted abbeys and born-again castles William Henry Fox Talbot needs more than a parenthesis. Arguably he is the most influential man to have worked from such a background. Certainly he is one of the most interesting.

The technical details of his achievements as a pioneer of photography are more easily read about than thoroughly understood –

Fox Talbot's window, Lacock Abbey

24

Lacock

Fox Talbot collection, Lacock

26

by the layman, that is – but at least the results are fully accessible. A print of the earliest negative in existence – his – faces its subject, the oriel window, in the South Gallery at Lacock. The original, ghostly and powerful, can be seen in the Science Museum at South Kensington. There is a permanent exhibition of his work in a converted barn, now the Fox Talbot Museum, that stands at the abbey gates. And when it comes to background reading Gail Buckland's *Fox Talbot and the Invention of Photography* could hardly be bettered.

Fox Talbot was not, of course, the only master of a stately home to use the money and leisure and influence that his position brought him to develop his own personal genius. The same was true of Sir Edmund Harry Elton, the nineteenth-century potter who owned Clevedon Court, Avon. The parallel was in fact very close. In the first place, it takes only a slight stretch of pigeonhole to insert Clevedon Court as a born-again castle, for, though it was built at the period most scorned by Sackville-West when manor houses had no longer any real need to be fortresses as well, it does have several defensive features. More importantly, Fox Talbot and Elton themselves were alike in that they both had considerable general gifts from which their principal talent emerged. The relative value of the general gifts is debatable: is it, for example, more of a contribution to be an expert Assyriologist and an FRS, as Fox Talbot was, or to invent an automatic gas lighter and a device for keeping women's skirts out of bicycle wheels, as Elton did? But the value of the main creative drive of each man can hardly be compared with that of the other; they were both true originals.

Although Fox Talbot was not born at Lacock and did not go there to live until 1827 when he was twenty-seven, he seems to have experienced an immediate empathy with the property which he had inherited as a baby. It was there that he conducted his first photographic experiments, and, naturally enough, it was *his* abbey – lawn, cloisters, stable court, trees, sheds – that provided the background for early portraits of *his* establishment – wife, daughters, sisters, gardeners, labourers. The building appears in his book *The Pencil of Nature*, 1844–5, of which the Athenaeum said: 'The experiment of photographically illustrated books is now before the world.'

With all his aptitudes and skills people seem never to have called Fox Talbot a dilettante. They were right. And when it came to photography – his most brilliant aptitude and farthest-reaching skill – his dedication was obviously total. For him it was both the present and the future, as must have been realised by whatever friend or relative suggested he should call one of his daughters Photogena. (He did not follow the suggestion.)

He made no parade of his personality but throughout his life he had a steely sense of identity. When he was thirteen he wrote in his diary: 'I have travelled 6,959 miles and this is the 4811 day of my life.' He died at his beloved Lacock at the age of seventy-seven, no doubt in full knowledge of how many miles he had travelled and how many days he had lived.

Chapter 2

WHERE PARADISE WAS

ONCE UPON a time Paradise simply meant a garden. As the universe got more complicated the word gathered up many other notions, mostly connected with religion and with temporary or eternal bliss, until at last it came to imply an almost total absence of plants.

The idea of the garden, the bright and beautiful enclosure, seems always to have had connotations of superior spirituality. Francis Bacon thought that it was not just aesthetically but morally better to create a garden than to build a house. His essay 'Of Gardens', though in too many paragraphs it degenerates into a seed and bulb catalogue, contains striking statements of this point of view.

> A Man shall ever see that, when Ages grow to Civility and Elegancie, Men come to Build Stately sooner than to Garden Finely, as if Gardening were the Greater Perfection.

This suggestion may throw some light on the fact that, in England at any rate, man has always been much readier to destroy gardens than houses. Gardens will grow again. He can always arrange for more. It is like re-uttering his most effective spell or prayer; and he can use a new translation if he wishes, to bring it all up to date.

Such destructiveness is today viewed with varying degrees of tolerance. Miles Hadfield roundly says: 'The English have been the most dreadful garden vandals.' Graham Stuart Thomas agrees in principle but tends to make the best of things:

> I think it natural to value most those gardens which show, unadulterated, the style in which they were created. However if one can forget the puristic approach, one's senses can glory nonetheless

in later additions and accept them as the taste of successive generations.

He points out that, as the art of planting can never be static, gardens 'are particularly susceptible to fashion and to the passing of time, if the two things are not synonymous'.

Nobody, however philosophical about it, could dispute the fact and the extent of the destruction. Miles Hadfield rightly says that when it comes to National Trust properties there is not a single house 'built between late Tudor times and the early part of the eighteenth century which stands in its original garden setting'.

Very occasionally and in special circumstances this does not matter. Mompesson House and its garden are an example. The house was built in the Cathedral Close at Salisbury in 1701 by Charles Mompesson whose ancestors had lived in an earlier house on the site for nearly seven decades, and redecorated forty years later by his wife's brother, Charles Longueville, with the most fetching plasterwork on the ceilings and staircase walls. There was a small garden at the back of the house bounded to the north by the fourteenth-century wall of the Close which had been built partly with stones from the old town. The wall is still there, authentic and ancient as can be, so however much and however many times the garden has been changed, the space it has occupied must always have been the same and have borne the same relationship to the house.

So the present garden, laid out during the ownership of Denis Martineau who bought the house in 1952, fits in well, although it corresponds with no period in the house's previous history, certainly not with the elegant formality of gardens during the post-Restoration years when it was built. It consists of a lawn with surrounding paths and herbaceous borders, all well kept, such as might be found in any prosperous London suburb, provided the owners had taste and no hankering after terrible effects and features. Yet somehow it extends the charm of the house. It must be a question of scale.

It cannot be a question of size, for one of the most imposing mansions in the land, Montacute House, Somerset, built by Sir Edward Phelips in the last decade of the sixteenth century, has almost as good a relationship with its present garden – planned and planted by William Phelips in the nineteenth century – as the relatively tiny Mompesson House. This needs some explaining. It

Plasterwork, Mompesson House

could be that there are enough traces of the original garden to establish some real idea of what it looked like: the enchanting pavilions on the east side where the entrance used to be; the raised walk surrounding the garden on the north side. These give a stimulus to the imagination, and so, though more subtly, do such recent plantings as the border of shrub roses which include varieties known to have been popular in the early days of Montacute. It helps to know their names: one of them is Red Damask; it was brought from Damascus by Crusaders in the fifteenth century and settled healthily in England.

Some of the features which have not survived are a much greater loss than others. I particularly regret the mount, which stood in the middle of the sunken garden on the north side and which was shown on a map of 1774 before being replaced some years later by a pond. I have nothing against ponds and cannot agree with Bacon that they 'marre all, and make the garden unwholesome and full of Flies and Frogges'. It is just that a mount was so characteristic of the Elizabethan garden, and so necessary to the owner's full pleasure. Apart from a few of his high windows, it was the only place from which he could look down, godlike, and appreciate the beautiful patterns he had created.

The chief reason why the relationship of house and garden at Montacute is so right is, again, the scale. The house is vast and so is the garden. Each part of it is at the same time so exciting and so restful that one is never daunted by, is not even conscious of, its whole extent, but in fact from north to south – that is from the far end of the sunken garden to the far end of the Cedar Lawn – it measures three hundred yards which was unusual for an Elizabethan garden. Its shape has not altered much since the house was built so we still get the advantage of these beautiful proportions.

Another reason is that later generations of planners and growers have respected the spirit of the house; or it has imposed itself on them. There is a bravura about Montacute which is echoed even by the most misguided performances of some of Sir Edward's descendants, such as the drive on the west side of the house. This approach was part of the improvements undertaken by the eighteenth-century Edward Phelips to show that he had brought a new prosperity to Montacute. These included a new west front to which the new drive was to lead; the main entrance had originally been on the east side. About both drive and entrance Edward Phelips made a martyr of himself, complaining about Arduous

Undertakings at his Age as though he had carried them out with his own hands. Perhaps he tried too hard. The drive is too long, too straight and too melodramatic (and nowadays, though this is the fault not of Edward but of William Phelips, too full of Victorian yews) and conjures up some old illustration of a lone knight galloping towards a castle on a particularly foolish Quest. It is nevertheless a great act of showmanship, in the authentic style of the founder.

His swashbuckling attitude has come down through three centuries and more, and influenced many who have worked and advised in the gardens. The plantswomen concerned have been especially resolute characters. Phyllis Reiss who earlier this century made a wonderful success of her own garden at Tintinhull House, not far away, helped with the borders in the east court of Montacute. Her theory being that only strong colours could stand up to the yellow stone of the house, not content with using them herself, she replanted the borders which had been filled with subdued flowers and foliage by no other than Victoria Sackville-West. Few would have dared. And on a previous occasion, with a boldness which approached bloody-mindedness, Gertrude Jekyll took it upon herself to disapprove of the two beautiful little pavilions.

Montacute House, west front

Ultimately, I think, it is the reciprocity between house and garden, once achieved and afterwards respected, that not only survives all changes but justifies them. Montacute House is surrounded by gardens which were and still are supportive to it, and which it seems to protect. One might think of Barrington Court, Somerset, as an example of the opposite. Gertrude Jekyll's garden, beautiful and original as it is, has no relationship, spatially or spiritually, with the house. It is more like an exhibit which is being given an honourable place in the grounds. In spite of Jekyll's contempt for Victorian gardens they are more in keeping with centuries-old mansions.

Time has little to do with this mutuality. In the south drive of Montacute, by which most visitors nowadays approach the house, there is a Monterey cypress, the largest in the country, planted something like a hundred and fifty years ago, and sharing the height and dignity of the house. Opposite it is a row of feathery light-green bushes which make no sense until you look inside them and see the wide base of a tree trunk with shoots sprouting out of it. They mark a kind of resurrection. Before the Second World War they were really fine Canadian redwoods. When war came and

Yew hedges, Montacute

Montacute House

wood was needed they were summarily chopped down. And then this inadvertent coppicing took place. Now both the full-grown cypress and the mutilated but vigorous redwoods are part of a harmonious settlement.

The other day I was walking on the Cedar Lawn, which lies south of the original entrance on the site of an early orchard. It was a grey afternoon and, though everything was looking very lovely, the colours all seemed to be shades of one muted nameless one. The cedar of Lebanon and the blue cedar, and the chestnut tree with its swirling baroque trunk, were distinguishable by their shape rather than by any version of green or brown. The ancient yew hedge which over the years has slumped down into layers and rolls which suggest a fat idol relaxing, was only a darker version of the overall tone. Suddenly the sun came out. The house went gold, the blue cedar went blue; just what one would expect but for the strong impression that a common switch had been clicked.

Water plays very little part in the present garden at Montacute. It meant everything to the seventeenth-century gardens at Dyrham Park, Avon. In 1686 William Blathwayt, a senior civil servant, married Mary Wynter, the heiress of Dyrham. After two years she came into her inheritance and almost immediately her husband set about transforming, to the point of completely rebuilding, the existing manor house. At the same time he started improving the garden, under the guidance of the famous George London.

Dr Johnson, writing with his usual blistering good sense about the garden which Alexander Pope had constructed at Twickenham, pointed out that 'as some men try to be proud of their defects' so Pope when he needed a tunnel under the road made a grotto of it. Something of the same positive attitude applied at Dyrham. Nature provided William Blathwayt with a steep hill on the east side of his house and a great deal of water that had to be got down it somehow. So he made a terraced water garden.

Our ancestors regularly prayed for a good water supply but William Blathwayt must have been embarrassed by his. It is still unusually prolific as has been proved in various droughts. Indeed the site of Dyrham Park was a strange place to build a house, in spite of the beautiful view to the west – over level land to the Welsh hills – for the slopes on the east side of the house are really high and both the visible streams and the invisible must have drained right down into it. Part of one's first impression of Dyrham today as one enters the park from above and looks at the house far

Dyrham Park

below is how damp it must be. More robust generations than ours apparently felt the same. The eighteenth-century writer on rural matters, Stephen Switzer, records the impression of the man in the lane:

> The Quantity of Water which abounds here and plentifully supplies the Waterworks is found fault with by some Persons as an Annoyance to the House, seated low.

He himself feels that the drainage system is adequate.

The cooling effect of water in a garden can never have been really necessary in England with its few hot days, but the sight and sound of it might well have been a blessing; particularly perhaps the sound. Gardeners have always been alive to the noises, often the voices, of a garden. Gertrude Jekyll could tell what trees she was near when her sight was almost gone.

> The birches have a small, quick, high-pitched sound; so like that of falling rain that I am often deceived into thinking it really is rain, when it is only their own leaves hitting each other with a small rain-like patter. The voice of oak leaves is also rather high-pitched, though lower than that of a birch. Chestnut leaves in a mild breeze sound much more deliberate; a sort of slow slither. Nearly all trees in gentle wind have a pleasant sound, but I confess to a distinct dislike of the noise of all the poplars, feeling it to be painfully fussy, unrestful and disturbing. On the other hand, how soothing and delightful is the murmur of Scotch firs both near and far.

Neptune, Dyrham Park

The sounds of water at Dyrham must have had an immense range of pitch and tone and volume. The noise on the east side would have been deafening. Switzer said that 'it very near equals the Billows of a raging Sea, and may be heard at a very great Distance'. I am sure it could, and that travellers on the Bath road listened out for it. The system started at the top of the hill with a cascade which came tumbling down about two hundred and fifty steps, accompanied by a line of supportive jets which Switzer vividly described as a 'Slope-Walk of Fountains'. At the bottom of the hill, the water smoothed out into a canal, but its conventional murmurs, if any, would have been lost in the general roar.

On the west side it would have been another matter, with the noise of the cascade muted by the bulk of the house. The main body of water having passed under the stable block emerged at the front of the house greatly tamed, so that the sound of the little waterfall – melodramatically called a cataract – which fed two ponds would have seemed like gentle splashing. The ponds themselves, said not to have altered all that much from that day to this, are placid and apparently motionless, though the water rushes rowdily away at the far end of the garden.

Alexander Pope thought that gardening was a more truly godlike act than the writing of poetry. As he did both so well he must be allowed the comment, and anyone conjuring up the glories of the garden at Dyrham in those early days would at least admit a connection between the two talents. Kip's famous engraving of Dyrham published in 1712 in Sir Robert Atkyns's *Ancient and Present State of Glocestershire* and Stephen Switzer's descriptions in his *Ichnographia Rustica* in 1718 together give a breathtaking picture of this great paradise, with its intricate and elegant layout, its inspired planting, its parterres and avenues and terraces, its gilded wrought-iron and statues and topiary.

It had only a century of life. When William Blathwayt was working at his outdoor improvements he groused as much as Edward Phelips of Montacute ('I know the aversion mankind has at Dyrham for *finishing* anything') but he did not realise that the fashion he was following, though still much admired, was already in decline. For years it kept going as a respectable eccentricity, and the wonders of Dyrham were a byword for several decades. But gardens and parks were changing all over the country. The new ideas of the eighteenth century and those of Capability Brown in particular eventually swept everything away. At Dyrham a local trendsetter started the process of destruction and Humphry Repton came down to administer the coup-de-grâce. The east garden has reverted to parkland.

The parkland is beautiful, but for serene contemplation of it there are too many poignant traces of what has been lost for ever. Neptune still stands at the top of the hill where the cascade started. Except for some dilapidation he is exactly as Switzer described him:

> cut out in Stone, of large Dimensions, with an exalted Trident in his Hand; a Whale is represented between his Legs, discharging a great Quantity of Water into Basons on the Heads of Tritons, from whence it falls in large Sheets to the Pond.

The pond has gone, the trident has gone, and in the context of

Dyrham Park

plain dry grass the god's handsome, amiable face seems to wear the dignified bewilderment of a cat when it wakes up and finds its patch of sun has moved. Down below, signs of the clearing and banking-up of soil, organized by William Blathwayt ('When will this levelling be at an end?') to accommodate the flat part of the garden, without the end product look like mindless tinkering with the lowest slopes of a graceful hill.

The west garden was more subtly disfigured, in that it was turned not into parkland but into another sort of garden, of roughly the same extent. The two ponds are still there but modified in shape to suit a different taste. The lower pond was given a wavy outline to avoid the reactionary horrors of a perfect oblong, and the top pond a municipal cosiness quite foreign to London's geometrical style. Both have a large central shrub which acts as a prettifying island. The walks have disappeared, though the ghost of the main avenue asserts itself as a long low hump in the middle of the present lawn.

The garden of The Courts, Holt (a village in Wiltshire with an unusually fine green), is entirely a twentieth-century creation which bears no relationship at all to the house as it originally functioned. The Courts, a handsome, basically seventeenth-century stone building, is said to have been a tribunal where weavers brought their disputes for arbitration. As such its setting would probably have been a court-yard, appropriate to a public building which provided for a great deal of coming and going on the part of the administrators of justice, and of overwrought litigants whose object was to get in and out as quickly and successfully as possible and who had neither time nor inclination to dally round lily ponds.

The house was converted into a dwelling in early Victorian times but it was not until the Edwardian decade that the garden came into being. The owner at that time, Sir George Hastings, organized the layout. There were no natural features such as a slope or a river to guide or limit him and not much established planting. He had seven acres of flat meadowland to do what he liked with. The only reservation to this freedom was that whatever he did the house would remain tucked into the north-east corner of the grounds, set sideways to them, and no more integrated than by the very Edwardian loggia that he built on to its south side.

In a way this open opportunity must have been a greater challenge than was faced by Lady Cecilie Goff who with her husband took over The Courts in 1920. Like a sensible woman she also took

Deer-proof planting, Dyrham Park

The Courts, Holt

over the framework of the garden that Sir George had created: the system of paths, the hedges, the topiary and the garden buildings. Then, like a highly imaginative woman, she brilliantly transformed the whole, though not in a manner that would have distressed Sir George. They were both sensitive gardeners of the early twentieth century and had both come under the influence of Gertrude Jekyll; Lady Cecilie in particular was a fervent admirer of hers.

Other members of the Goff family carried on this sympathetic development. In the 1950s Miss Myra Goff planted trees in a meadow that encircles the garden proper and is divided from it by a gracefully undulating hedge: Sir George's. It is not an arboretum in the grand way of Bicton and Westonbirt – the trees have only had thirty years to grow – but it is extremely pleasant.

A third thing which Lady Cecilie took over from Sir George was his collection of stone statues, a replica of those he had installed in the garden of Ranelagh House, Barnes. They provide many of the surprises which she, following Gertrude Jekyll, believed a garden should offer, and have a great deal to do with the personality of her garden.

Since men first started writing about gardens they have paid considerable attention to the presence in them of objects other than plants, and statues have come in for particular scrutiny. In 1485, Alberti, the great authority on Renaissance architecture, gave it as his opinion – in words that sound like the reverse of the old smoking-room joke – that outdoor statues should be absurd but not obscene. He liked statues in gardens to be slightly ridiculous, and the rich dukes of Italy who followed his lead had a fine line in funny dragons, humorous tortoises, and Roman soldiers being caught up in elephants' trunks.

The statues at The Courts do have something comic about them, either intrinsically or as a result of their placing. In the middle of the south lawn is an over-tall pillar surmounted by the over-small head of a man twisted sniffily away from the house. At the end of an avenue sits a leopard (I think; it could be a dog but its nose is feline rather than canine) rising from a nest of ivy, opposite a stone pot which balances him neither in size nor in soul. Across the north end of the brimming rectangular pond a path leads, roughly, up to a sculpted head on a plinth, set so asymmetrically as to suggest that something went wrong. On the way back to the house, at the sides of a short flight of steps and next to a handsome false acacia, are two couchant lions, delightful, but too small and too cheeky

The Ambulatory, Horton Court,
near Dyrham Park

for their situation.

The many ornamental stone containers are fairly predictably placed and comparatively unremarkable except for the pot supported by some very come-hither (in a Pears Soap kind of way) caryatids in the centre of the sad remains of a pergola. The garden buildings are pretty – especially the little conservatory – rather than surprising, though it is almost surprising that the classical pavilion should, in an English garden, face north.

The garden ministers to most known fantasies and presents others which have been up to now unsuspected. 'The garden's full of furniture. And the house is full of plants': the 'House and Garden' song made famous by Flanders and Swann was outdone by this garden even before they sang it. It *is* a house, with rooms and doors and windows: an unpredictable house with hidey-holes and secret places.

One October afternoon a dog is rushing about in the fallen red leaves of the arboretum, amiably showing off with a big branch between his teeth. The berries of the holly hedge and of the cotoneaster bushes are brilliant and so are the huge heavy flowers of the red fuchsia. Everything in the garden is not only rosy but scarlet.

*Clifton Suspension Bridge, and
Frenchay Woods*

Chapter 3

THE ECHOING GREEN

BLAISE HAMLET is bogus and beautiful. It is appropriately set in an estate which is just as beautiful and in some respects equally bogus. Blaise Castle itself came first. It was built in 1766 for the merchant Thomas Farr, on the crest of a hill four miles north of Bristol, and was quite frankly a folly. Its three circular towers, arranged in a becoming triangle as was fashionable at the time, never defended anybody or were attacked by anybody, except perhaps on grounds of taste. They did, however, attract the tourists who drove out from Bath at the time of its heyday in great numbers, especially the young people who were not there for the waters in the first place.

About Blaise Castle House, built in 1796 by William Paty for John Scandrett Harford, the Quaker banker, there is, essentially, nothing bogus whatever. It is a good-looking house, unaffected and almost austere, which suggests both the banker and the Quaker. But it has its moments. One of them is a romantic rather foolish little thatched dairy, designed by John Nash; too close to the house: even a token cow would have been a launching-pad for smells and flies.

The other exuberance is Humphry Repton's approach to the house. The long carriage drive that winds up through the gorge alongside a stream which in those earlier days may have rushed down it is superbly unnecessary. Anybody wishing simply to call on Mr Harford would have nipped in from the public road, on the same level, and been received at the modest though dignified entrance that visitors to today's museums still use. But, in having guests approach through the gorge, Repton was stunning them with his favourite precepts. Wooded hills were his signature, not bare ones with a clump on top like those of his master Capability Brown. Water was to stay in the bottom of the valley, not tumble picturesquely down from the heights. These ideas in themselves may sound prosaic but the theatricality which came from Repton's early passion for the stage, and his later experience of it as play-wright and designer, carried him through to effects which must have made unsuspecting visitors, winding upwards and onwards between the stark white cliffs that emerged every so often from jungle vegetation, think they were heading for the Castle of Otranto at the very least.

In 1807 John Harford bought a six-acre piece of land in the nearby village of Henbury. It was called Greens, and it was a village green that Harford had in mind. The green had originated, quietly and practically, as a central clearing in an Anglo-Saxon settlement, intended for communal discussions and as a place to protect the old, the young, the weak and the four-legged against enemies. By the end of the eighteenth century it had become a focus of nostalgia and romanticism, as in Blake's poem, written in the 1780s.

Old John, with white hair,
Does laugh away care,
Sitting under the oak,
Among the old folk.
They laugh at our play,
And soon they all say:
'Such, such were the joys
When we all, girls and boys,
In our youth time were seen
On the Echoing Green'.

Wessex villages tend to be nuclear or linear rather than 'green' as in other parts of the country, so the idea of deploying houses round a stretch of grass was slightly unusual in the first place, and the green which John Nash and George Repton, son of Humphry, established, departed even further from tradition, in shape; it was not the time-honoured triangle, it was hardly a geometrical figure at all though it fitted into a rectangle; and it had the wavy outline loved and much used by Capability Brown. In use, originally, it must have departed furthest of all. The idea that the cottages were made to face in different directions in order to discourage neighbourly gossiping is no doubt apocryphal, though as an idea it would have been consistent with the interfering paternalism of

Blaise Hamlet

the times; the motive was probably love of asymmetry for its own sake. All the same it is clear that nothing very much was expected to happen on the green, or rather the lawn, of Blaise Hamlet; nothing traditional anyway. The tenants were to be retired servants of the Harford family: too frail by now to protect others, too old to wrestle or dance round the Maypole, too poor to attract pedlars, and too remote and small an audience for mummers and jugglers or even for a mystery play.

There was always a civil pretence of life on the green at Blaise Hamlet. Early Victorian engravings are at pains to include not only a person so ancient as to have no gender sitting on a bench, but also, say, a trim young matron accompanied by a child. The child is never rampaging about but being prettily helpful, at the pump, for instance. It was in the best tradition of the Picturesque that cottage-dwellers should be decorative. John Claudius Loudon, who summed it all up in his authoritative *Encyclopaedia of Cottage, Farm and Villa Architecture and Furniture* which began to appear in 1832, confidently expected that 'there would always be children playing and villagers passing to and fro, to contribute to the rural effect of the scene'. An earlier arbiter of the movement, William Gilpin, had also regarded as essential 'the occasional group of villagers supplying an additional embellishment to the landscape'.

But even if a group of elderly servants, who would certainly not have retired prematurely, could hardly have provided much indigenous go, there were perpetual invasions from the outside world, right from the beginning, for Blaise Hamlet made a very considerable impact, on both Englishmen and foreigners. It is true that excursions regularly came out from Bristol just for the frolic, as they had come from Bath to see the Castle, but the majority of visitors were serious, well-informed people, who wanted to learn something.

They must have learned a great deal. Building cottages for employees and tenants was something that landowners had conspicuously been doing for more than a hundred years, but increasingly their methods had come under fire. As often as not the new houses, of uniform design, were strung out on both sides of a road, and by the last decade of the eighteenth century, though most people agreed as to the end, this was widely felt to be the wrong means: lazy, obvious, insipid and unsuitable to the countryside. In *Essay on the Picturesque*, 1794, Uvedale Price, whose name and views are usually coupled with Gilpin's, was eloquent in his criticism of such deadly regularity. But it was one thing to criticise and another to come up with a viable alternative. Some ill-advised things were done, on both sides of the argument, between the first stirrings of dissatisfaction and the building of Blaise Hamlet.

This was begun in 1810. The village green of Nash and Repton took up only part of the six acres Harford bought, but they fitted nine buildings round it; ten dwellings, for one was a double. Each was different, and in almost every possible way. Even lovers of the Picturesque might have felt that though they had prayed for variety this was ridiculous. The roofs were varied, in both shape and material; only three were thatched, strangely few at a time when everybody was being so lyrical about thatch, and the rest were tiled. Two gable-ends had holes suggesting a dovecote. Not only were the cottages set at apparently random angles, but each front door was in a different place. The windows were different, the chimneys were very different, in both placing and pattern. Even the lean-tos, sheds and privies were given personalities of their own. And, as a final touch, the naming was not consistent; most of the cottages were called after flowers and plants – Jasmine, Rose, Vine – but there had to be discrepancies, so one indicated shape – Diamond – and another its accommodation – Double.

There was something slightly perverse about the green itself, apart from its shape. Traditionally the village green had many attributes, some punitive – the stocks, the ducking stool, the whipping post – others more positive – the horse trough, the pump, the pound for stray animals. Blaise Hamlet had only a pump. Certainly any of the other things would have been most inappropriate in the circumstances, but a solitary pump does look artificial. Nash and Repton doggedly followed their star: the pump is placed asymmetrically. They were not responsible, of course, for the inscription carved on it later by Harford's son in praise of his father's liberality, but it is curiously in keeping. Strong in emotion and weak in syntax it is in itself a single-handed gesture against the age of reason.

The point about Blaise Hamlet is that it carries total conviction. It is not in the least surprising that visitors came and still come, and that its impact is felt to this day. As housing it is bogus. There is no sign of any thought for the people who were to live there or any idea that they might prefer a less poky sitting room to an imposing chimney or more light to gracefully overhanging eaves. But in being beautiful, unique and of powerful personality it is one of the wonders of the world, of which there are far more than the time-honoured seven.

Yet I often imagine – impertinently – a sadness about the place. The octopus of suburbia is flopping and heaving close by and might poke its tentacles through the trees at any minute. And twentieth-century notions of lower-case picturesque have actually got inside. The last time I was there I saw a cartwheel in one of the gardens, and a white-painted wrought-iron whatnot – a sort of plant tray on fixed wheels – in a porch, and dinky little flower beds outside a front door where, as the 1826 lithograph shows, none was intended. There is a feeling of something coming to a close, which makes the last verse of Blake's poem seem more relevant than the jauntier ones.

> The sun does descend
> And our sports have an end.
> Round the laps of their mothers
> Many sisters and brothers
> Like birds in their nest
> Are ready for rest
> And sport no more seen
> On the darkening green.

Selworthy Green, Somerset, though it is modelled on Blaise Hamlet, is surprisingly unlike it, in both appearance and atmosphere. This may be because there was a different motivation behind it. The land-owners who planned the earlier new villages and hamlets were at least as much concerned to show that they could afford it as to improve the lot of their dependants. In the course of the nineteenth century, genuine and often whole-hearted philanthropy began to creep in.

George Eliot wrote *Middlemarch* in the early 1870s but the action takes place forty years earlier, and Dorothea, the heroine, represents the new way of looking at things. The first time she really appears in the novel she is concentrating so intently on a drawing that only with difficulty can she join in her sister's talk of jewels, and the drawing turns out to be a plan for model cottages which she wishes to put up on her wealthy uncle's estate. She is quite untrained, and charmingly diffident about her design: 'I shall think I am a great architect if I have not got imcompatible stairs and fireplaces.' But in fact she is as well-prepared as any male land-owner could be, for she has acquired Loudon's book, which could only just have come out, and studied it, as very probably she had studied earlier pattern books too of which there were a multitude, some sane, some crazy.

There can be no doubt about Dorothea's motive. She is always sincere, and never more so than when she exclaims:

> I think we deserve to be beaten out of our beautiful houses with a scourge of small cords – all of us who let tenants live in such sties as we see round us. Life in cottages might be happier than ours, if they were real houses fit for human beings from whom we expect duties and affections,

or than when her sister, speaking of the cottages, has commented, 'It is your favourite *fad* to draw plans,' and she almost shouts, '*Fad* to draw plans! Do you think I only care about my fellow-creatures' houses in that childish way?'

By the time George Eliot wrote, the fictional Dorothea would have acquired counterparts in real life, for the female philanthropists had arrived. Indeed – to step outside the book – in her second marriage she would have met and perhaps worked with them. There were differences of temperament: Dorothea went about her mission gently though ardently; Lady Waterford, Miss Georgina Talbot, Miss Mary Anne Talbot and Baroness Burdett-Coutts were all battleaxes. But the imaginary woman and the real ones had much in common, apart from the wealth and leisure which made their work possible. Their schemes were consistently governed by a wish that those they were re-housing should be as healthy and comfortable as possible. There was no emphasis on appearance for its own sake.

To mix literature and life once more: in *Northanger Abbey* when Catherine is visiting Henry Tilney's parsonage and admires a cottage in the grounds, his father General Tilney, mistakenly thinking she is an heiress, immediately says:

> You like it. You approve of it as an object. It is enough. Henry, remember that Robinson is spoken to about it. The cottage remains.

The cottage, due for demolition, is now to be kept, as a pretty object. Three or four decades later, Lady Waterford would never have preserved a decrepit insanitary cottage, however picturesque, or have thought of it as an object. For her, the preservation of mere

Selworthy Green

prettiness needed, as she once said, 'mixing up with a more onward march'.

This more onward march reached Selworthy quite early in the century. The builder of these cottages, Sir Thomas Dyke Acland, 10th Baronet, was a friend not so much of John Harford senior as of his son, so although Selworthy Green was created only eighteen years after Blaise Hamlet, the influence of a second generation was already at work. And as Acland did not employ an architect there was nobody to stand between his own notions and the final result.

He was a conscientious man and read all the right things. It is pleasant to know – rather than to surmise – that he had a thorough working knowledge of P. F. Robinson's *Rural Architecture*, one of the best of the pattern-books, which appeared in 1823. A copy full of his own underlinings and annotations was found in his library and can still be seen.

He must have agreed with Robinson that cottages should be 'objects of interest' and 'picturesque features in the landscape'; it would have been too outré not to, in those days. And, when it came to including the cottagers themselves in the effect, he and his wife went even further than some by dressing the pensioners up in scarlet cloaks. This sort of thing was done in other planned villages: at Old Warden in Bedfordshire the cottagers, it is said, were issued with red garments to match the paintwork. But no Acland went so far as to put them in pointed hats, as sometimes happened elsewhere.

To be part of an idyllic scene and gawped at by tourists might I suppose have gratified one or two modest egos, but not many, probably, especially when it became obvious, as it soon would have, that cows and sheep were being headed down specific paths so as to be in the production too.

Yet Selworthy Green does look less self-indulgent than Blaise Hamlet. The whole effect is not so formal and alien; the picturesqueness is not so resolute, more affectionate. In fact the cottages look very like what most people expect pretty cottages to look like. They are placed with conscious asymmetry, certainly. They are in many ways ornate – decorative thatch, decorative tiles, latticed windows, oriel windows, gables and porches – but not in every way: the chimneys though tall are perfectly plain. It is arguable whether or not they could properly be called *cottages ornés*, whereas there is no doubt that the Blaise Hamlet houses have to be.

Selworthy Green has natural advantages. It stands on a slope, and there is a church at the top, both very important elements in the picturesque. It was, and still is, integrated with an attractive village. There is no suburban sprawl nearer than Porlock.

Two of the Selworthy houses are open to the public, one as a National Trust shop, another as a café – the rooms are relatively light and large – so there is some realistic coming and going on the green. People cross it to strike into the paths that burrow through the woods. Sometimes a thatch is being repaired, and then they pause to watch and appraise, exactly as our ancestors must have done. They knew more about it, of course, and had less time to spend on the way to their own work, but they must have screwed up their eyes and pointed in much the same way, and made remarks. This green still echoes.

Chapter 4

DU CÔTÉ DE CHEZ ACLAND

FROM Dunkery Hill on a clear day when the sea, 1,705 feet below, is bright and hard, and Selworthy Church on its very English hillside looks as white as a Moroccan villa, the terrain is so magnificent that it made Henry James even at ground level feel that he needed nothing less than the pen of Mr Addison. In fact his own pen was perfectly adequate:

> I beheld . . . breezy highlands clad in the warm blue brown of heather-tufts as if in mantles of rusty velvet, little bays and coves curving gently to the doors of clustered fishing-huts, deep pastures and broad forests, villages thatched and trellised as if to take a prize for improbability, manor-tops peeping over rook-haunted avenues.

On a misty day it is like the motorway poster warning drivers that there are lorries and trucks in the fog ahead. Momentarily you seem to overtake the view, then it speeds on into the mist again. Yet all the time it makes its presence felt. The indicator near the beacon that shows you what you could see if it was visible is tantalizing but not irrelevant, even on the worst day. Its pointers mark a real enough journey: to the coastal towns and inland mountains of Wales, back across the Bristol Channel to Weston-super-Mare, down the M5 to Brent Knoll – which to most people is a Rest Area rather than an Iron Age camp – to the seaside resorts of Somerset, and right round to Yes Tor in Devon that stands at the beginning of a grander, greyer waste-land than Exmoor. The indicator is only literally up in the clouds; it not only mentions a Rest Area but an international airport and a nuclear power station as well.

Approaching Dunkery Beacon in the mist

From the top of Dunkery in any weather you can either trace or imagine the war-track of the Doones, along which they rode on the night that John Ridd, returning from his school in Tiverton to the family farm at Oare, crossed their path for the first but not the last time. They were on their way home from a raid at the ancient port of Watchet on the Somerset coast. No two people can agree as to which valley the Doones' actually was, but the outlaws would certainly have been riding westwards towards the Devon border, with half their journey done. As they were travelling slightly south as well as west they would have turned inland soon after Dunster, and as they were dependent on Dunkery Beacon to light them into the folds of Exmoor, their warpath might well have lain along the Horner valley.

The beacon on Dunkery is probably as old as fire, and burned for pagan festivals and secular alarms so long before the approach of the Armada and the celebration of the present Queen's jubilee that it makes the latter two events seem contemporaneous. It was a bold stroke on R. D. Blackmore's part to have the seventeenth-century Doones monopolise the beacon to light themselves home. No watchman dared kindle it for any other purpose; the only one who attempted it found himself on top of his own bonfire.

Young John Ridd had had a bad day. The murder of his father by the Doones had not been openly mentioned by John Fry, the servant who had come to fetch him, but enough dark hints had been dropped to curdle anybody's blood. As the travellers left the shelter of Dulverton in its wooded valley the fog came down on Exmoor and they had to find their way by the 'mellow noise, very low and mournsome', of a gibbet where a sheep rustler was swinging. Two miles from Dunkery they fell silent and listened 'as if the air was a speaking trumpet' for they had come to the place where their route crossed the Doone-track. They were just ascending on the far side when a red light sprang up from the beacon, which could only mean that the Doones were on the warpath.

Now the beacon was rushing up, in a fiery storm to heaven, and the form of its flame came and went in the folds, and the heavy sky was hovering. All around it was hung with red, deep in twisted columns, and then a giant beard of fire streamed throughout the darkness. The sullen hills were flanked with light, and the valleys chined with shadow, and all the moors between awoke in furrowed anger.

59

Dunkery Beacon

From Dunkery Beacon

The Doones went by. Neither Blackmore nor his young hero saw them as lithe, high-souled adventurers, intent on the benevolent re-distribution of wealth. They were selfish louts whom nobody loved.

> The flinging fire leaped into the rocky mouth of the glen below me, where the horsemen passed in silence, scarcely deigning to look round. Heavy men, and large of stature, reckless how they bore their guns or how they sate their horses, with leathern jerkins and long boots and iron plates on breast and head, plunder heaped behind their saddles, and flagons slung in front of them; more than thirty went along, like clouds upon red sunset.

The Doones have gone – though occasionally their spiritual descendants set fire to the gorse – and an air of magnanimity rather than pillage blows over and around Dunkery. The paths are not warpaths and are named after the Acland family and local worthies who were their friends. They suggest innocent triumphs and family holidays and good weather: Cat's Scramble, after a favourite horse nicknamed the Cat which belonged to the second wife of the 11th Baronet; Boys' Path, after the 4th Baronet and his brother, who must have been very little boys at the time for the younger died at the age of seven.

The naming of one of the paths was an act of positive reconciliation. Sir Thomas Dyke Acland, who became 11th Baronet in 1871, had not done as well in his parliamentary career as might have been expected. He was a member of parliament on and off for most of his life but his voting for the repeal of the Corn Laws in 1846 had spoilt his prospects for the general election of the following year and had in consequence disrupted his political future. When in 1892 his third son Arthur was made Minister of Education (and education had always been one of Sir Thomas's specialities) with a seat in Gladstone's cabinet, his generosity of spirit must have been severely tried, especially as he was still furious with Arthur for having resigned holy orders and a family living a decade before. Yet he dedicated a path to him and his achievement. How unlike the homelife of the Doones.

Of these paths my own favourite is the one which starts from Webber's Post, a clearing in the woods at the top of the long steep hill out of Horner, and follows the northern contours of Dunkery Hill from east to west for about two and a half miles: Dicky's Path. The track is grey and gritty but brightened by pink patches of red sandstone. It is low enough for the walker to look up at the cairns on the skyline that mark the Bronze Age barrows of Robin How and Joaney How, and high enough for him to look down on Horner Wood and see what in earlier ages everybody walking at a certain height would have seen: the wonderful green roof which covered the country, and under which nearly all its inhabitants lived.

For most of the way the hillside is covered with heather. The path is scalloped in shape; it curves from combe to combe, dipping down sharply into each of them. There are three: Hollow, Aller and Sweetworthy. Their streams run into East Water which joins Horner Water to the north. As the track crosses them everything turns green for a few yards. When the cuckoo is in England its call comes ceaselessly across the valley, sounding so pagan that even a single cockcrow strikes a Christian note.

The Aclands were never a boastful family but they were suitably confident. They had a strong sense of inheritance, and many baronets must have stood on Dunkery Hill in clear weather and said to their sons, 'One day all this will be yours.' It was indeed a heritage to be proud of.

The Aclands settled in Devon near Barnstaple in 1155. Nobody knows where they came from – it may have been Flanders – but for four centuries they steadily grew in consequence, property and wealth, marrying girls with famous Devon names such as Rolle and Cruse, farming with increasing success, and, in the fifteenth century, rebuilding their house, Acland Barton. It was the usual history of contenders at that time, the alternative to vanishing without trace.

The first really significant expansion was when John, younger brother of Hugh who had inherited and stayed on at Acland Barton in the middle of the sixteenth century, moved south and bought a property near Broadclyst where he prospered the more flamboy-antly of the two. The next heir was Hugh's grandson, John, who was to become the first baronet. On his succession he decided to make the estate near Broadclyst the main family seat, while keeping on Acland Barton; and he bought the manor of Killerton, also in the parish of Broadclyst, for his mother.

The outcome of the Civil War brought the Royalist Aclands low, though it was in the volatile course of it that John Acland had been baroneted. But, helped by a series of marriages that were prudent to the point of brilliance, the family soon struggled up again. And even further up: in 1745 the 7th Baronet married the spectacular heiress Elizabeth Dyke who brought in not only a fortune and her name

Exmoor and Dunkery Beacon

Exmoor

but three extensive properties in Somerset, one of them being the Holnicote estate. Holnicote is on Exmoor, and the 7th and 9th Baronets became the staghunting Aclands, unable thoroughly to concentrate on anything alive or dead that had no antlers on top of it.

The 10th and 11th Baronets changed all this. They were at heart as well as in chronological fact men of the nineteenth century. They shared its increasing social awareness and its growing conviction that politics should be conducted more seriously. They kept abreast of new ideas in education, to the extent of actively pioneering certain schemes, and of new ideas in religion which they carefully weighed up before making their personal decision. All these attitudes their descendants took over from them as they, in their turn, led the way into and through the next century.

On his succession in 1898 the 12th Baronet, christened Charles Thomas, asked to be known as Sir Thomas rather than Sir Charles, as the name conveyed a greater sense of continuity, linked him unmistakably with the Devon and Somerset estates, and ruled out any confusion with the Johnny-come-lately Acland baronets (his own close relatives but it was the principle of the thing) in Oxford. His attitude on this point shows a patriarchal inflexibility which must have made the events of his regime particularly painful to him. He had to face more changes than any of his ancestors.

He inherited as a wealthy man who could comfortably afford to do up the house at Killerton in lavish style and re-design the grounds. But the family money came mostly from farm rents, and the Edwardian age was a bad time for agriculture. Most of the Devon property was productive and easy to manage, but half the Holnicote estate was moorland, and moorland of far greater intractability than the western stretches of Exmoor which the Knight family had, with some degree of success, struggled to tame in the early nineteenth century.

For the first decade of the century life seemed to go on much as usual for landowners – with someone employed to comb the dog, and a footman in a cockaded top hat waiting at the railway station – but the cliffs were crumbling. The rich were being increasingly taxed, death duties were going up, there was talk of a land tax, employers were having to pay for national insurance stamps and subscribe to pensions. Then came the First World War.

The 12th Baronet may have been a patriarch but he was essentially a benevolent one and seems not to have resented the moves towards social justice that hit his own pocket so hard. Neither was

The Caratacus Stone

Holnicote Estate, above Horner

he wholly inflexible; he showed that he could think imaginatively and strongly even in a storm of change. The outcome of his thinking was announced in a letter to *The Times* on a winter day in 1917 when the papers were carrying news of U-boats and of Ypres and heartbreaking casualty lists. The writer of the letter was the Earl of Plymouth, Chairman of the Executive Committee of the National Trust; and his subject was 'a very interesting and important gift' to the Trust: a 500-year lease of seven or eight thousand acres of Sir Thomas's Exmoor property. One fears that on a day like that people might have been too far gone in misery to see how interesting and important it was; but they have since.

The new property, the letter explained, would not be a possession in the ordinary sense of the word, neither would it be a source of income to the Trust. It would, he hoped and believed, be better than that.

> We believe that in agreeing to take this new departure, and, for the first time, accept something less than ownership, the Trust is finding a new and useful means of discharging its duty to the nation: and that many generations of Englishmen who will visit Exmoor in the future will gratefully remember the name of Sir Thomas Acland, whose forethought and generosity preserved for them one of the most beautiful pieces of wild country to be found in England.

West Luccombe Packhorse Bridge

All this took place; and more, for a precedent had been provided. When Sir Thomas arranged his bequest the National Trust was something new, so new that the Exmoor acres more than doubled the property it controlled. The 12th Baronet was well ahead of his time but his example was followed, and within his own family too. In 1944 his great-nephew Richard gave both the Killerton estate and the Holnicote estate to the Trust and now his name is gratefully mentioned as well by more Englishmen and women than the Earl of Plymouth could have foreseen as they go for walks along 'Acland's way'.

The Holnicote estate now consists of 12,420 acres. Of the half which is not open moorland, about two-thirds are farmland and one-third is woodland. Its northern boundary is the sea of Porlock Bay and the Bristol Channel. To the west it stops just short of the town of Porlock and the further slopes of Exmoor that stretch on into Devon. Its eastern border crosses the fertile valley that leads towards Minehead. At the southernmost point is Dunkery Gate which is the entrance to Dunkery Hill.

Horner Bridge

Holnicote House, after its third fire and consequent restoration, is no longer the focal point of the estate as it once was. The village of Selworthy has taken its place socially, and visually too, for its white church catches the eye in a way Wordsworth would have thought very damaging to the general view but which for the rest of us makes it a helpful landmark.

The villages and hamlets of Holnicote are beautiful, though strangely small in a dominant landscape. West of Selworthy they stand in a curving line under North Hill: Brandish Street, Allerford and Lynch, with Bossington at the end, so near the sea that its red ploughland looks unnatural. Across the valley under the slopes of Exmoor lie, more at random, Horner, Luccombe and West Luccombe. Farther to the east is Blackford, and farthest of all, Tivington, near where the estate begins. Among them they have every charm: thatched cottages, an old corn mill, a fifteenth-century church, a sixteenth-century chapel, a dovecote and three packhorse bridges.

The terrain is so varied that management has to be versatile. The farms of Porlock Vale need very different organization from the more challenging hill farms, especially those of Exmoor. As an Edwardian guide picturesquely put it: 'Exmoor is still untamed after all the efforts of agriculturists to comb its shaggy coat.'

Allerford Packhorse Bridge

Diplomacy of a high order has to be practised when it comes to the replacement of lovely old farm buildings, but people are obviously much readier to ring out the old when the new that is rung in is of such a high standard as, say, the new farm buildings at Tivington, so well designed, so handsome. The diplomacy has to be of an even higher order when it concerns the *siting* of new farm buildings, but crowded and articulate public meetings such as the one recently convened by the inhabitants of Luccombe and attended by a posse of National Trust officials come down from London do give everybody a chance.

'We're aesthetic too' was the headline of a *Sunday Times* feature in the summer of 1984, and it did seem to show that the attention the Trust pays to appearances is not only acceptable but coveted. Deyan Sudjic, Architectural Correspondent, begins his article – and indeed continues it – in spirited journalese:

Allerford is one of those Somerset honeypots that has the power to drive whole convoys of coach-trippers into frenzies of snap-taking. It boasts a lovingly restored medieval packhorse bridge, flanked by clumps of mellow stone cottages, every one of which seems to have been turned into a guest-house or a retirement home . . . It is the kind of place in which every lawn is manicured, and in which even the public lavatory, disguised as an oxblood-red barn, is architect-designed.

The point of the article, and of the headline, is that a council estate of the 1950s, which forms part of Allerford but was excluded from supervision, instead of rejoicing in its independence *wants* to be stopped from ever painting its houses bright blue, *wants* to be part of a conservation area.

Chapter 5

CHEQUERED SHADE

YOU ENTER a Site of Special Scientific Interest and find yourself in one of the loveliest wildest woods in the country. One of the oldest, too: Horner Wood had almost certainly taken on its present shape and size by Domesday and it has an air of relaxed permanence which suggests that it will be there, like Drake in his hammock, till the great Armadas come.

The best way in is from Pool Bridge at the top of the wood, high up the slope of Exmoor and not far from open moorland. As Horner Water enters the trees, at the beginning of its three-mile descent to Horner village, it is neither as brown nor as choppy as a Dartmoor stream, but it has the same headstrong air and looks equally cold: men point to the pools in which, or in others just like them far away, they bathed in youth. The path goes down beside it, though sometimes the river lights off on its own and becomes nothing but a sound. Towards Horner, East Water with its tributaries comes down from Dunkery Hill to join it, and as the ground levels out, the two waters enter the village as a broader, quieter stream which flows sedately north to Porlock Bay. One of its banks is planted with walnut trees which, though said to be hollow at heart, look safe and tame compared with the oaks of the wood.

Most of Horner's nine hundred acres are covered with oaks. There are other trees, too: beech and alder and birch, with a few patches of hazel and rowan, and ash on the wetter ground. But oak is dominant. It always has been and there are plans that it always will be. There is little oak woodland on Exmoor, and the Horner oaks have always had rarity value. They were once prized for their bark which was used in tanning. Nowadays they are esteemed for their looks and for the part they play in conservation.

71

Oaks, Horner Wood

'Dead wood' is a damning metaphor; most professions are said, at least by their younger members, to be full of it. As a literal fact, however, it is life-giving. Bugs thrive on it. Some birds, like the redstart, nest in it. Horner Wood has more fallen trees than I have ever seen in one area anywhere else. Not that their rate of collapse here is greater than the national average; it is simply that unless the dead wood is blocking the path or the river, it is not economically feasible to remove it. And, on the principle that if life hands you a lemon you can make yourself a lemonade, the difficulty has become a bonus. It is a pleasure to see the redstart. And recently when I watched two enormous paradisal beetles, with shining carapaces and confident bearing, walking – not frantically scuttling – along the path, I thought that was a pleasure too.

People of a certain temperament – the best, in my opinion – will find that the dead wood makes Horner more impressive rather than less. One tree has plunged down the slope headfirst and lies like that with its roots high above it. One is stretched across a clearing, where the sun now enters for the first time in centuries, and leaves a huge circle in the canopy which once its crown filled. Their attitudes and their size and grandeur recall the defeated gods and angels of poetry, most of whom, when they fell from on high, fell into woods. This has always been a potent symbol. Milton, out of orthodoxy, made his rebellious angels land in a lake of fire but he really imagined them

Thick as autumnal leaves that strow the brooks
In Vallombrosa.

Keats was entirely single-minded when describing the fallen Titans.

Deep in the shady sadness of a vale
Far sunken from the healthy breath of morn,
Far from the fiery noon, and eve's one star,
Sat grey-haired Saturn, quiet as a stone,
Still as the silence round about his lair;
Forest on forest hung about his head,
Like cloud on cloud. No stir of air was there,
Not so much life as on a summer's day
Robs not one light seed from the feathered grass,
But where the dead leaf fell, there did it rest.

Both Satan and Saturn would have looked perfect in Horner Wood.

The chief overthrower here is the wind, not old age or failing powers, presumption or pushy rivals, though of course they come into it too. The cyclone of December 1981, dreadful as it was to all of us living in these parts, hit Horner directly: the whole storm – still centre and all – whirled right through the wood. The damage it caused, especially on the east-facing slopes, was so widespread that clearance *had* to be done. Three years later a local timber merchant is still to be seen, systematically carrying out the work.

This destruction took place in a few hours, but every winter the prevailing wind keeps at it, scraping away the tops of the higher trees. Even in the summer it frequently flicks a whip, and with an alarming capriciousness. On a day as still as the one Keats described, when the ferns are motionless, one frond will thrash wildly for a moment and then go quiet again. And suddenly a little wave will leap up from a smooth stretch of water, like a miniature white horse.

Most of the dwellers in Horner Wood are hardly ever seen by those who walk along the path in daylight. I have never come across a fox or a badger there, nor even, surprisingly, a squirrel. Yet they are present somewhere. Neither have I seen, in or above the wood, the buzzards or the tawny owls that are well-established residents, or the herons that visit. Once, some of the inhabitants were human beings. Right down by the river, towards Horner, the remains of a building are buried in shrubs and undergrowth. It may have been a mill. If so, the miller, if only half-buried at the time, must have lived a strange invisible life.

The most discussed inhabitant of Horner Wood at present is the mink which has invaded the whole system of streams. They are interlopers and are talked about in terms appropriate to any alien species, anywhere, in any age. They certainly act as outsiders are assumed to do: they eat the natives' food; they take over the natives' work; their cultural differences put the natives off. Attempts are being made to get rid of them but they seem unnaturally determined to stay. I have a vision of a chorus line of land agents and foresters addressing the careless mink-farmers or whoever was responsible for the invasion.

> Take back your mink
> To from whence it came.

Even I see sheep and deer in Horner Wood. The sheep barge

Oaks, Horner Wood

about on the slope, dislodging rocks with apparent petulance. The red deer pick up their feet delicately and put them down choosily. They all come to graze. There are no grazing rights; they are said to come there by tradition, which is a gracious way of indicating that they cannot be kept out. How indeed could they be? Ideally, of course their presence should be discouraged for their nibblings do interfere with re-growth.

Not far from the ruins of the mill is a memorial stone: STAGHOUND RECORDER KILLED HERE SEPTEMBER 10 1882. Let us now praise famous hounds by all means, but some there be which have no memorial in the wood: the stags. Yet, before getting too indignant at the injustice, one must not forget such accounts as the following passage from a letter written on Exmoor in 1759.

> This noble chase being ended, my Master his brother and Mr Brutton with about 20 gentlemen more waited on Sir Thomas Acland at Pixton where each of them drank the health of the stag in a full quart glass of Claret.

Much good it did him, but it was a gesture.

There has been staghunting in Horner Wood since the Norman Conquest and many local squires like the eighteenth-century Aclands have been obsessive about it. It is estimated that today there are three hundred deer based on the wood, which is a third of the deer population of the whole of Exmoor. When the staghound pack was disbanded in 1825, deer numbers fell to fifty in thirty years. The argument that hunting protects the hunted is of course a familiar one that has been used about many animals ever since man felt a need to justify his behaviour in this respect. There must have come a moment when the Missing Link said it about the mammoth.

Anyone looking down on the apparently flawless canopy of Horner Wood from the surrounding hills might guess the unbroken look to be deliberate. So it is, part of its management policy being that areas of felling and clearing shall remain as few and small as is consistent with renewal. The same onlooker might then suppose the wood to be unusually dark inside, and, strangely, it is not. Very rarely does the shade look other than green, sometimes very bright green.

Just below Pool Bridge the valley becomes sharply V-shaped and continues so for at least two miles. To see the sky even very

Beeches and Douglas Fir, Horner Wood

intermittently at the top of the steep slopes on either side you have to tilt your head well back. Yet light picks out the gigantic ferns, prints shapes on the path like early Fox Talbot photographs, and X-rays fish in the stream. You may be standing in shadow yourself but there are always patches of radiance on the leaves beyond.

Green is of course the predominant colour, but not the only one. The soil is poor – much of it is the Hangman Grits which form the northern part of Exmoor – and it gets poorer as the slopes rise; but with the high rainfall and the influence of the sea there is a wet warmth, in the valley bottom at least, which makes plants grow quite theatrically. The foxgloves are large and brilliantly purple. The honeysuckle is almost luminous. The bracken turns into polished copper. In the combes and clearings and above the path there are fine butterflies. I saw two Small Whites and two Meadow Browns that seemed to jump in and out of a current of air like dolphins.

Even the greens and browns of the tree trunks are richly and significantly varied. The Horner Wood lichens are internationally important and indeed are the reason for their habitat's becoming a Site of Special Scientific Interest. There are nearly a hundred and sixty different species, and no doubt an expert eye would see a hundred and sixty different colours.

About two miles down from Pool Bridge the wood changes character. The valley bottom flattens out and the path widens as it goes into the lower woods. At the top of the walk much of the right-hand cliff gave the impression of parkland hanging on a slope, like a rug on the wall instead of on the floor, but now that side of the valley recedes and loses height.

The wood turns towards the north, and it is here, as the left-hand side begins to face due east that the full extent of the storm of 1981 is painfully apparent. At least it would be painful if such careful replanting were not being carried out. The new trees begin life in protective tubes. The first set of tubes to be used was white, and these when glimpsed out of the corner of one's eye look like a field of gravestones at the end of *Oh! What a Lovely War*. The next phase of replanting has used light brown tubes which are much less startling.

The last few hundred yards of the wood bear signs of the outer world. Meadows come alongside on the right. The public comes in at the gate and the path is full of those who never walk more than a few hundred yards. The cream teas and the car parks, the lavatories and the leaflets are within reach.

Selworthy Wood is as different from Horner Wood as it could possibly be. It is neither ancient nor spontaneous. A view of North Hill painted in the eighteenth century shows it as almost completely bare of trees, with cultivated fields reaching more than halfway up the slopes. Today woods rise behind the village of Selworthy to cover its southern side and extend along the range as far as the village of Allerford.

The greater part of this new wood can be dated almost precisely, for it was the creation of one man who celebrated ten separate events. The first plantings would have taken place in 1809 and the last eighteen years later. What happened between these two dates was the birth of ten children to Sir Thomas Dyke Acland, 10th Baronet, and his wife Lydia. Each baby was welcomed with a plantation.

Sir Thomas took possession of his estate in 1808 at the age of twenty-one, his father having died fourteen years earlier. He then married Lydia Hoare, a relative of his mother's and a connection of the Stourhead Hoares. As he and his wife naturally settled at Killerton it might have seemed more appropriate if the trees had been planted there, but Sir Thomas had been brought up at Holnicote, as his widowed mother had remarried and settled there, and he loved it.

Horner Wood bears no real trace of any personality but its own. Paths that impinge on it and have been given Acland nicknames – Lord Ebrington's Path, Granny's Ride, Tucker's Path, Cabinet Walk – shrug them off as modern liberties taken with ancient tracks. Selworthy Wood on the other hand is unashamedly eloquent of the 10th Baronet, the nineteenth-century family man who liked to proclaim his choice of wife, his choice of Sunday morning walks and even his taste in hymns, psalms and conversation.

His tribute to Lady Acland must have been well worth having. As Lydia Hoare, she had been used to beautiful grounds wherever she visited, and Mitcham Grove, her father's estate, had accustomed her to the very best. At the heart of the wood she married into, two paths converge on Mitcham Seat, an obviously affectionate replica of a feature of her childhood home. It is a charming thatched arbour, a sophisticate's version of a primitive hut, with tree trunks for pillars, and a complicated double roof which looks as though Robinson Crusoe had been whiling away a very long weekend.

The view from the arbour is wonderful. Beyond fields of the

barley that does so well in these parts, and over the fertile valley, lies Horner Wood, tamped down into its cleft in the hills, filling it full, but without seeming to lose any of its springiness. Behind and above it spread the grey folds of Exmoor. Much of the same view can be seen at any point in the whole width of the wood. It is like looking out from a long arcade.

There is only one main path through Horner Wood. In Selworthy Wood there is a network of paths, zig-zagging and criss-crossing. It can be very confusing but the 10th Baronet needed great variety for the walks he took with his family between one Sunday service and the next. In the heyday of both Sir Thomas and the wood there were forty miles of paths, complete with red-cloaked pensioners to sweep them.

There are oaks in Selworthy Wood but they do not dominate as they do in Horner. Sir Thomas also planted chestnut, Scots pine and silver fir. And in 1815 – it must have been for the birth of Henry – he set a large plantation of ilex at the seaward end of North Hill. Henry became Regius Professor of Medicine at Oxford, was baroneted and lived to be eighty-five, but he was a lucky baby if only for this wood.

Ilex must be one of the most interesting trees in the world. It looks both northern and southern at the same time. The leaves and the trunks are Corot green, and in this plantation there is no other colour at all, simply an underwater effect. There is no undergrowth; the ground could be sterile. When the leaves fall, which happens all the year round as these are evergreen oaks, they immediately lie pale and dead. The formation of the trees is startling. The terrain rises to a steep dome and, as you look up, they stand like the Medusa's hair. At eye level they suggest another mythical woman, Daphne; the slender branches reach up like fingers, not straining or clutching so much as having divinely turned into something else.

In the summer of 1984 the *Sunday Times* magazine launched a Greenwood Campaign. Bows and arrows were not provided; we were expected to 'save our ancient woodlands' by sending donations for this purpose, with a target of £10,000 in mind. The air was loud with slogans and epigrams ('If you go down to the woods today you are much more likely to hear a chainsaw than a songbird') and much vilification of the 'factors responsible for bringing the ancient woodlands to their knees'. Behind all the verbiage there was a great deal of good sense and sound argument.

In principle, that is. The next week's correspondence column contained ripostes – from the National Farmers' Union and two highly respected landowners – which, in being thoroughly specific and therefore open to check, showed that the Friends of the Earth, who had supplied most of the material for the article, had spoken inaccurately, confusing acres with hectares, describing as ancient woodland certain plantations which were no such thing and glowing with righteous indignation about forests which were in no danger at all.

The article was accompanied by a map dotted with black numerals that indicated where dreadful things were going on. Northwest Somerset was densely speckled, but the point is that not even the Friends of the Earth could put a black spot on the woods of the Holnicote estate.

Horner Wood has been shaped and administered by man since medieval times, perhaps even earlier days, and from 1745 when it came under the care of the Aclands it continued to be intelligently managed, especially by the 10th Baronet who looked after it and his new plantations on North Hill to the best of his very considerable ability. Today the Holnicote trees, given to the National Trust in 1944 along with the rest of the estate, are in even safer hands, for their welfare could not now depend on personal caprice, as it might have done in the past if their former administrators had been less scrupulous.

There is a well-thought-out policy and an agreed plan. All considerations, however valid in themselves, such as financial profit, are now secondary to social and aesthetic concerns. The woods are there for the public to enjoy and they are there to be as healthy and beautiful and conducive to the well-being of the life around them as they can. The commercial aspect is not ignored but it gives way. Timber is felled and sold but not to an extent that would leave a hole in the canopy and often not at a time that would fetch the best price.

Chapter 6

MORE FOR THEIR ASSOCIATIONS

Days seem to dawn, suns to shine, evenings to follow, and then I
sleep. What I have done, what I am doing, what I am going to do,
puzzle me and bewilder me. Have you ever been a leaf and fallen
from your tree in autumn and been really puzzled about it? That's
the feeling.

T. E. LAWRENCE wrote these quiet sad words from Clouds Hill a
few days before his death.

His cottage stands in a forest of rhododendrons on the slopes of
Clouds Hill, a mile north of Bovington Camp. In his day the road
up from the camp was half the width it is now; fewer and smaller
tanks went past, and the heath was not yet totally devastated
by gigantic exercises and manoeuvres. Even nowadays there is
something like silence round the house; rhododendrons have a
muffling property that neither church bells nor high seas can get
through. In 1923, when Lawrence first rented the cottage, the peace
must have been profound.

The house is not large – two up and two down – but many of us
have been successfully brought up in homes as small, and I feel
that the guide books do go on rather about its littleness. They tend
to call it modest, and this euphemism is not even precise, for the
place has an air of confidence.

Some of the comments made about it are downright sour. James
Lees-Milne in *Prophesying Peace* calls it 'a pathetic little shoddy place'
and adds for good measure:

The visitors have stolen all they could lay hands on, including the
screw of the porthole window in Lawrence's bedroom, and the
hasps of the other windows. The bunk gives an idea of his asceticism.

This is not even logical. The bunk, if it proved anything, would not prove that Lawrence practised asceticism but that he expected his guests to, for he mostly slept on a wide sybaritic leather bed downstairs. Earlier in his book Lees-Milne brings on Bernard Shaw to back him up: 'He liked the idea of our [the National Trust's] holding T. E. Lawrence's Clouds Hill, for "it is good for nothing else".'

Animosity towards a house is not difficult to explain when its tenant has such a strong personality as Lawrence. People's feelings about him do tend to rub off on to his home and these feelings are often hostile, for he can make men uneasy and he can make them envious. The envy may be something like the resentment that Eliot's Gerontion acknowledged so openly: envy of the warrior.

I was neither at the hot gates
Nor fought in the warm rain
Nor knee deep in the salt marsh, heaving a cutlass,
Bitten by flies, fought.

Whatever the cause, I cannot think of any public figure who has inspired so much bitchery as T. E. Lawrence or so many comments which provoke the reflection that it takes one to spot one. The spite, which of course does not in every case spring from the speaker's own inadequacy, is variously based and often memorably worded. Extracts would provide strong material for a kind of Satanic book jacket.

A sonorous fake as a writer (Kingsley Amis)
A bore and a bounder and a prig (Henry Channon)
Nothing but a great man (Aldous Huxley)
The last right-wing intellectual (George Orwell)
An odd gnome (Aubrey Herbert).

However undersized, Clouds Hill is the house in which Thomas Edward Lawrence, or Chapman or Junner or Ross or Shaw, turned into Lawrence of Arabia. He is buried in Moreton churchyard nearby and from his wide and beautifully-lettered tombstone under the yew tree nobody could guess he had been anything of the sort. His only graven title is Fellow of All Souls, Oxford. There is no curved dagger, no camel's saddle, not the ghost of a flowing robe; these attributes are all to be found in Eric Kennington's effigy of him in Wareham church. Oxford has officially won; at Lawrence's

Clouds Hill

feet is a marble book inscribed with the University's humble yet vainglorious motto: Dominus Illuminatio Mea.

A look at the main dates of his biography show how small a part of his short life had anything to do with the Arabia of his popular title. His distinguished career in Arab countries before the First World War, studying the language and engaged in excavation, and the time he spent in Oxford writing up his expert findings, could never have made him Lawrence of Arabia. Only his wartime activities did that.

He once described his part in the First World War as 'the sideshow of a sideshow'. Since then historians and military experts have accorded him a much more central place, and indeed there were times when he himself seemed to think that he was the Big Wheel. There is no doubt that the masterminding of the Arab revolt against the Turks did have very far-reaching consequences. What they were exactly I am not competent to assess, and in the context of Clouds Hill it is not necessary to try.

For as much as a quarter of his life Lawrence either occupied or owned Clouds Hill. He first rented it in 1923 as an occasional retreat from the Royal Tank Corps, which he had joined, as Private Shaw, after his discharge from the Royal Air Force, where for a few months he had been Aircraftman Ross. Even after he left Bovington Camp behind, on re-joining the Air Force in 1925, he still kept on the house; indeed he bought it, and for the next ten years spent as much time and money as he had on repairing and improving it: putting in a bath and so on. With firelight and candlelight it must have been truly inviting.

Clouds Hill

Certainly guests came, both when he was there and when he was not for he was generous with his company and his property: family, literary friends, fellow soldiers: what one of them called a mixed grill. E. M. Forster was an item in the grill and has written affectionately, as many others have done, of the conversation and the music (rolling from the huge round mouth of the E.M.G. gramophone) and even of the picnic meals: finger food and no alcohol.

Clouds Hill did not change Lawrence much. In 1918 he wrote: 'When they untie my bonds I will not find in me any spur to action.' He was saying more or less the same thing in 1935: 'There is something broken in the works, as I told you: my will, I think. In this mood I would not take on any job at all.' After seventeen years he had not recovered from his war, which had been strange and punishing to an unusual degree. The dangers, the exertions and the hardships had been of no conventional kind. The swashbuckling aspect of his duties (exotic lands, alien companions, foreign tongues) and the childish element too (fancy dress, de-railing other people's trains) when integral to affairs of great seriousness must have fazed even such a manifold character as Lawrence.

In the early years of peace, his transformation into Lawrence of Arabia did not help. His achievements had been genuine, but his legend was the work of an American lecturer, Lowell Thomas – anxious to create a British hero – several fashionable portrait painters and a great many silly schoolgirls. He realised all this of course, and to an extent enjoyed his status, but at a time when he was feeling, with reason, that the cause he had fought for had been betrayed, it seemed like mockery too. During the very years when he was preparing *Seven Pillars of Wisdom* for publication he could hear songs of Araby even through the rhododendrons.

Yet Clouds Hill did restore him, for he loved it. The Greek motto which he inscribed over the door (variously translated as 'Why worry?', 'Don't care' and 'Nothing matters') declares a worried, caring man to whom many things mattered. But his home did calm him. At the time of his retirement from the RAF when he was looking forward to living there permanently he called it an earthly paradise.

I have never had such a strong impression that the owner of a house was still present, after death, as I have in Lawrence's; to be truthful I have never had the impression at all before. Apparently friends who survived him have said they keep expecting him to come in at the door. I understand, but my feeling is that he has already come in at the door. I hope he stays; he seems to be at peace.

Thomas Hardy's cottage is west and slightly north of Clouds Hill, not far from Dorchester. The two men were friends at the time Lawrence was living in Dorset. Although Lawrence died only seven years after Hardy, when he was born Hardy was already forty-seven. But this difference of age did not hinder their responding well to each other. Hardy, unlike the Gerontions of the world, showed that he was captivated rather than vexed by Lawrence's life of action and the experiences that were so remote from his own. Lawrence in his turn tolerated and even subdued ('perhaps by some esoteric desert magic' suggests Robert Gittings) the terrible dog Wessex that was one of the several banes of the second Mrs Hardy's life.

All this took place at Max Gate of course. Yet it is Hardy's birthplace at Higher Bockhampton that is usually mentioned in the same breath as the home of Lawrence's last years, the grounds being that they are both architecturally undistinguished, not very old – early nineteenth-century – and are cherished 'more for their associations'. (Coleridge's cottage in Nether Stowey is often put in this category too.) As the associations of both buildings are outstanding, the phrase is less dismissive than it may sound.

Hardy's cottage is picturesque certainly, but no more so than thousands of small farmhouses and homesteads in Dorset and East Devon. It looks much older than it is, for Hardy's great-grandfather built at the end of a long tradition which started in the early sixteenth century. In later life Hardy always exaggerated its charms, size, number of outbuildings, and the *comme il faut* deportment of the neighbours.

The opening sentences of *The Life of Thomas Hardy*, ostensibly written, but actually typed out from notes, dictation or a script, by Florence Emily Hardy and dedicated by her to the Dear Memory, is like the beginning of a weighty historical novel:

Hardy's Cottage

> *June 2, 1840*. It was in a lonely and silent spot between woodland and heathland that Thomas Hardy was born, about eight o'clock on Tuesday morning the 2nd of June 1840, the place of his birth being the seven-roomed rambling house that stands easternmost of the few scattered dwellings called Higher Bockhampton, in the parish of Stinsford, Dorset. The domiciles were quaint, brass-knockered, and green-shuttered then, some with green garden-doors and white balls on the post, and mainly occupied by lifeholders of substantial footing like the Hardys themselves.

It is obvious from these comments alone that the Dear Memory was a fearful snob. His own words betray him. After all, a seven-roomed house cannot ramble very far. The substantial footing of the Hardys could only be maintained by the sacrifice of scores of relatives who were workmen and servants, so he sacrificed them. His first wife Emma was a snob certainly but she cannot be held totally responsible for this; it seems to have been a natural instinct of Hardy's. It cannot have brought him much happiness, yet there is comedy for everybody else in this melancholy man's dogged policy of pretending not to see his lively working-class relatives. In *Young Thomas Hardy* Robert Gittings gives a very funny account of how Thomas and Emma used to ride through Puddletown.

The Hardys would bicycle stiffly through the main street, looking neither to right nor to left. Cottage doors were full of his close relatives, the Hands, the Antells, and visiting Sparkses; but Hardy neither gave nor acknowledged greetings as he pedalled resolutely on with Emma.

To disown his father and mother would have been going too far, even though Jemima had been a pauper-child and a cook. Hardy was always reasonably attentive to their needs and fairly regular in his visits to Bockhampton after he had finally left the cottage at the age of thirty-four to get married. He took Emma there though not for some time after the wedding, at which no Hardy was present. From hints which the bride dropped in middle-age she did not get on with her mother-in-law but she liked her husband's sisters, Mary and Kate, who had become schoolteachers. This was no great rise in status in the nineteenth century; as Mary grumbled to Emma: 'Nobody asks me to dinner or treats me like a lady.' But the grievance must have mollified Emma to whom it would have shown a sensible class-consciousness on Mary's part and a wholesome wish to better herself, which most of Hardy's other relatives cheerfully refrained from doing. One of the most interesting events at the cottage must have been when Hardy took Florence Dugdale there while Emma was still alive.

People are often disappointed by the cottage and feel that time and change have carried off the enchantment. They would prefer to find something more like the description in Charles G. Harper's *Wessex* which appeared in 1911.

> There, where the blue wood-smoke from rustic chimneys ascends amid dense foliage, and where the swart heaths begin, he learned his 'wood-notes wild'.

I suppose if you put it like that, the actual place is rather a comedown. But perhaps it is Edwardian high diction that has had a great fall, not so much what it is here attempting to describe.

The approach from the south through Thorncombe Wood is no doubt tamer than it once was but it is still romantically beautiful. 'Egdon' Heath to the east has been planted with conifers but from knowledge of other parts of Dorset it is easy to imagine what it was like when Tess walked across it from 'Weatherbury' (Puddletown) on her way to the Valley of the Great Dairies and in the exuberance of her new-found hope paused to sing 'O ye Sun and Moon bless ye the Lord, praise him and magnify him for ever'; or when Michael Henchard went there to die; or when Clym Yeobright returned:

> If anyone knew the heath well it was Clym. He was permeated with its scenes, with its substance, and with its odours. He might be said to be its product. His eyes had first opened thereon; with its appearance all the first images of his memory were mingled; his estimate of life had been coloured by it.

Certainly nobody will ever see again 'the great and particular glory' of Hardy's Egdon, or fully recapture the magic of these words:

> A Saturday afternoon in November was approaching the time of twilight and the vast tract of unenclosed wild known as Egdon Heath embrowned itself moment by moment. Overhead the hollow stretch of whitish cloud shutting out the sky was as a tent which had the whole heath for its floor.

But perhaps nobody but Hardy ever did see 'the great and particular glory'. There were always characters who, like Arthur Young when he first saw the heath, would exclaim, 'What fortunes are here to be made by spirited improvers!'

Nearly all the traits we now think of as essentially Hardyesque were the direct result of his environment and the kind of upbringing it involved. The tales Jemima Hardy entertained him with were a kind not usually heard at a mother's knee: suicides' graves and stakes through the heart. Indeed both his parents spoke freely to him of the brutalities they had witnessed in their own childhood. His preoccupation with hanging was certainly inculcated in extreme youth.

In *The Life* he speaks in a matter-of-fact way which would probably have surprised nobody who knew him of a hanging he watched, at the age of eighteen, through a telescope from the heath behind the house.

> One summer morning at Bockhampton, just before he sat down to breakfast, he remembered that a man was to be hanged at eight o'clock at Dorchester. He took up the big brass telescope that had been handed on in the family, and hastened to a hill on the heath a quarter of a mile from the house, whence he looked towards the town. The sun behind his back shone straight on the white stone facade of the gaol, the gallows upon it, and the form of the murderer in white fustian, the

executioner and officials in dark clothing and the crowd below being invisible at this distance of nearly three miles. At the moment of his placing the glass to his eye the white figure dropped downwards, and the faint note of the town clock struck eight.

The cottage was the centre of his life for over thirty years, in fact until the day when 'rising at four in the morning, and starting by starlight from his country retreat', he 'set out for Lyonnesse'. From it the family strolled out on their usual Sunday walk to Rainbarrow. To it he returned from visits to Puddletown relatives, running through the bracken in the evening mists, or from school expecting Apollyon to jump out from the trees. Not all his fears were bookish; once on Stinsford Hill he encountered two smugglers who were sitting on their kegs trying to look natural.

From babyhood he had a close affinity with the wildlife and the farm animals around the cottage. Sometimes he made the first move, one day going down on all fours in a field to eat grass with the sheep. Sometimes the wildlife did; his mother once found him curled up in his cradle with a large snake, both fast asleep. Perhaps the best example of his rapport with his surroundings is his experience on the heath (which found its way into *Jude*) when he was five or six.

> He was lying on his back in the sun, thinking how useless he was, and covered his face with his straw hat. The sun's rays streamed through the interstices of the straw, the lining having disappeared. Reflecting on his experiences of the world so far as he had got, he came to the conclusion that he did not wish to grow up.

Looking at the cottage from the west which it faces, it is easy to imagine, especially when the lights have gone on, how a party would have been there: the fiddlers, the skirts swirling, the open fire, and the cider barrel brought in from the woodshed. It is not so easy to imagine the composition of the early poetry and the first four novels even in the room where we know them to have been written. Fortunately *The Life* helps us with some vivid details of at least the practicalities such as the arrival of a letter from Leslie Stephen which, from its importance to Hardy at that stage, should have been delivered on a velvet cushion but in fact was found by a farm labourer in the mud of the lane where some school children had dropped it.

Desperate Remedies, Hardy's first published novel, appeared in

Lewesdon Hill, from Pilsdon Pen

1871. From the point of view of the actual writing its connection with Bockhampton was not very close for much of it had been done at Weymouth, but Hardy's experience of the *Spectator*'s savage review could hardly have happened nearer home.

> He remembered, for long years after, how he had read this review as he sat on a stile leading to the eweleaze he had to cross on his way home to Bockhampton. The bitterness of that moment was never forgotten; at the time he wished that he were dead.

In reality the *Spectator* review was by no means entirely hostile. Hardy made the most of its severity, and indeed was positively unjust, mis-quoting it in the *Life* as calling the novel 'a desperate remedy for an emaciated purse'. That is exactly the cheap sort of crack that a reviewer in any age might make but in fact the *Spectator*'s man did not make it in that precise form or without the accompaniment of hopeful talk about 'better things in the future'.

Soon however it looked very much as if the President of the Immortals had turned away to tease other young writers. In the course of the next three years *Under the Greenwood Tree* (quotations from poetry were fashionable as titles in 1872), *A Pair of Blue Eyes* and *Far from the Madding Crowd* (they still were in 1874) all appeared and were all praised by the critics and bought by the public. He had tried hard not to be coarse: with the backing of Leslie Stephen who advised extreme gingerliness in certain parts of *Far from the Madding Crowd*, he had picked his way through several minefields. Yet it was nothing so negative as caution that accounted for his success at this time; it was the positive result of living and working in the Bockhampton cottage. The environment of home inspired and strengthened his work. In 1874 he was ready to leave, to set up a home of his own.

The decision to bury Hardy's heart in Stinsford churchyard when his literary friends had bossily arranged to have him placed in Westminster Abbey was apparently a clerical compromise: Florence in understandable distress had consulted her Vicar. Hardy's siblings and close friends were shocked; the villagers got rather giggly. Yet there is a kind of appropriateness in the happening. Many poets and songwriters have left their hearts in San Francisco, felt them to be still in the Hielands, or asked to have them buried at Wounded Knee. It is in keeping with Hardy's greatness that the disposition of *his* heart should have been not figurative but literal.

Chapter 7

BUILDING GREATER

THE FOLLY of pulling down one's barns and building greater has never been put more powerfully than by the Bible: 'Thou fool, this night thy soul shall be required of thee.' But many poets have, in a less absolute way, taken up the theme. Andrew Marvell, anxious to praise his patron Lord Fairfax of Appleton House in Yorkshire, begins his poem about the property with the opinion that it is exactly the right size – unlike some – and he is scathing about any man who builds a bigger house than he needs.

> But he, superfluously spread,
> Demands more room alive than dead.
> And in his hollow palace goes
> Where winds as he themselves may lose.
> What needs of all this marble crust
> T'impart the wanton mote of dust,
> That thinks by breadth the world t'unite
> Though the first builders failed in height?

The beasts, Marvell points out, have always known better; their 'bodies measure out their place'. He singles out for praise the tortoise whose roof just clears his height. This is charming, though it is perhaps not very tactful to liken one's patron to a tortoise.

I cannot imagine what Marvell would have said about the Napper family of Tintinhull, Somerset; nothing probably, as his remarks about relative size were confined to the large-scale. The Nappers almost certainly did not read Marvell's poem. They cannot have heeded the Good Book either, for they did pull down their barns and build Tintinhull House; and lived happily for a long time after. The original farmhouse was Elizabethan but only just; about 1600

Fountain Garden, Tintinhull

is the date usually suggested. It belonged to the Nappers either from the start or quite soon after; they had lived in the village for several decades, at the handsome Parsonage, now the Court. It was obviously a pleasant house: long and one room deep with a cross-wing at the south end. But one of the young Nappers, probably Andrew, was a born developer, and at the beginning of the eighteenth century when he was twenty-seven he added a new west front and filled in the space thus left between it and most of the rest of the house.

No architect has been named as having designed the new façade, so none can be blamed. Whoever he was, he openly flouted the Orders, but in the hopeful way of a gifted amateur rather than in a spirit of grim and systematic anarchy. It is interesting to speculate as to his background, and tempting to think that he in fact consisted of Andrew Napper and his mason. The guide-book optimistically states that 'one is not worried by departures from strict Classical orthodoxy'. Oh, but one is, especially if one's husband is an architect and is accompanying one. Like Lady Bertram, 'guided by Sir Thomas' I could see that part of the entablature had been left out. And a basement window did suggest that somebody had misinterpreted the pattern book: the keystone was supported by a pier, which does seem a belt-and-braces affair.

The West door, Tintinhull

These things may affect the purity of Tintinhill House but not its charm, which is immense. The September afternoon we were there the sun came out after a grey morning. The house glowed like an apricot, and as the evening drew on I saw the full extent of the Napper flair and thoroughly realised the advantage a house has in facing west, provided there is no hill to take the last hour of sunlight. In this case there is none; Somerset comes up low and level to the garden. Right till the end of day the shadows lunge towards the house. The rounded box bushes become spearheads. The fish in the rectangular pool, if they are low enough in the water, send their shadows on ahead of them like torpedoes.

This is the trouble about all the criticisms of ambitious building: the result can be so very fetching. And nine times out of ten the motive is straightforward and sympathetic.

In the case of the Lytes of Lytes Cary, Somerset, the motive may well have been mixed. It must have been aggravating for our ancestors to bear – as so many did – a name expressive of some comic activity or personal peculiarity by which the founder of the family had been identified: Weselhedde, Brownejohn, Sadd,

Mutter, Foote, Hogge, Daundelyon, Freshfysshe, Lepper. William le Lyte must have been a dwarf if he was so much smaller than all the medieval men who fitted into those tiny suits of armour as to be called William the Little (unless he was so large as to make the nickname a flattering joke) and for some centuries his descendants acted in the pushy way that is supposed to be characteristic of little men or men who are simply called little. Fortunately in the case of the Lytes of Lytes Cary it took the form of extending their house.

Their behaviour in general was normal enough. From the middle of the thirteenth century onwards they went on record as having married heiresses, witnessed deeds, served as jurors, and as having been accused of crimes themselves while tirelessly accusing others of unspecified acts of knavery, villainy and foolery. Every so often a member of the family stood out from the rest: one fought at Agincourt, one wrote 'Abide with me', and two committed incest, though only according to the lavish prohibitions of the time and with an eventual pardon from the Pope.

At no time, as far as one can tell, were the Lytes social climbers. They were quite happy to be country squires. So were the Nappers of Tintinhull, apparently, though they did change their name to Napier. Both Lytes and Nappers simply wanted larger houses than they found and took steps accordingly.

The first recorded extension at Lytes Cary was an act of piety: a chapel probably built by William le Lyte's grandson Peter, probably in 1343. It originally stood alone, near the south-east corner of the house. Later development brought the house out to touch and partly join it, but there was never a communicating door: you had to slop along outside. There was plenty of surveillance, however; a window in the little room, imprecisely called the Oriel, leading off the Hall, had a good view of the entrance to the Chapel, while a rather saucy peephole in another little room that led out of the Oriel and into the Grand Parlour, gave a glimpse, through a glass darkly, into the interior of the Chapel. From outside, the Chapel still looks tacked on, a pretty annexe whose gable contributes very pleasantly to the overall pattern of the façade.

Peter's great-grandson Thomas, who succeeded in 1453, radically enlarged the Great Hall, but less than a century later he was to be completely outdone by his own great-grandson John. It was not just that John married a wealthy woman, Edith Horsey of Wiltshire. Most of the Lytes married prudently. As well as being rich the wives tended to be ambitious in a wholesome kind of way, and if

Tintinhull

99

Lytes Cary

The Pool, Lytes Cary

they became widows they contributed more than a mite to the work of aggrandisement. It was also the zeitgeist; a Tudor was now on the throne: Henry VIII. John Lyte was in a strong position: his ancestors had expanded and improved their lands as well as their house; he had money to spend on building, and royalty had made it the fashion. So he built, with an expansiveness that would have delighted the forefathers he outshone.

According to a seventeenth-century descendant who was a genealogist he 'newe built the Hall oriall, the 2 great portches, the closetts, the kitchen, and divers others places yet extant, with the dayrie house and the chamber over'. And this was not the half of it; there is no mention of the showiest item of all (unless it is included in 'divers others places'; it is certainly 'yet extant'): the south side of the house containing the Great Chamber and the Great Parlour; and they really were, and are, great.

The next two squires of Lytes Cary were clearly interesting and vigorous men but no builders. Henry Lyte, who succeeded in 1568, put his energy and imagination into being a herbalist, a horticulturist and antiquarian, and distinguished himself as all three. He was the Lyte of the best-selling *Lytes Herball*. He was also the Lyte who wrote *The Light of Britayne* which he presented to Queen Elizabeth when she led the state thanksgiving at St Paul's for the defeat of the Spanish Armada.

Thomas Lyte, another one, came next, in 1607. He was the genealogist who itemised John Lyte's building works. Though his true dedication was to genealogy he showed traces of his grandfather's passion: the panelling in the Parlour was probably commissioned by him and he certainly added the frieze in the Chapel which displayed the family coats of arms.

After this something entered the blood: not fatigue or inability to make money but what seemed like lack of pride in home. Only two or three generations later the Lytes were going out all over Europe, taking their *objets d'art*, such as a Hilliard miniature, with them. The last family marriage in Peter's Chapel was solemnized. Part of the house was conveyed to trustees. Then the estate was mortgaged. Then it was sold. Then it was neglected. When Sir Walter Jenner, the re-builder, came on the scene in 1907 he found the Hall a cider cellar, the Great Parlour a farm store and the Little Parlour a carpenter's shop.

Lytes Cary can never have been more beautiful than it is today. One autumn afternoon I stood at the beginning of the paved path *Stourhead*

*Whitesheet Hill, above
Stourhead*

Copper Beech, Stourhead Lake

that leads up to it between lawns and rows of clipped yews, chiefly looking but also listening to the first comments of other visitors as they came round the corner. The Lytes would have been interested. Nine out of ten people said pleasantly, 'Oh, it's not too big.'

I recently came across the following lively description of a house on the banks of the Mississippi in Jonathan Raban's *Old Glory*, and immediately thought of the Stately Homes of England.

> His father's house was a shack on the levee. It must have started out as a single room; then every few years someone added a new clapboard box to an end or side, so that it gave the impression of having gone on a drunken ramble round the riverbank. We kept on passing odd corners of it and eventually reached a front door.

In loftier terms this could apply to both Tintinhull and Lytes Cary. It also captures the spirit of a sketch made by John Aubrey in 1685 of Stourton House, Wiltshire, the building which Henry Hoare I pulled down in order to raise Stourhead in its place. It could not possibly apply to Stourhead.

The Stourtons were a prominent family from Saxon times, when Stourton House was built, to their eclipse in the early eighteenth century. For hundreds of years they married money, were returned to Parliament where they often distinguished themselves, served on important Commissions and held worthwhile posts at Court. Just like every family in a period of ascendancy they improved their house and extended their lands.

It was not until the reign of Henry VIII that their wheel of fortune began to shudder before its disastrous downward swing. The trouble started with a local, almost a domestic, feud. A neighbour and tenant, William Hartgill, was entrusted by the Lord Stourton of the day, the seventh by this time, with the management of his lands and the protection of his family while he himself went to live in Newhaven, simultaneously as Deputy-General for the king and lover of the daughter of the Countess of Bridgwater. In Newhaven he died, leaving a great deal of money to his mistress and none to his wife. His son, the eighth Lord Stourton, who was himself quite respectably provided for, could apparently do little about the mistress's inheritance but he could and did take it out on William Hartgill whom he dismissed with accusations of inefficiency and malpractice.

With sporadic flare-ups the inevitable resentment of both parties smouldered on into the reign of Mary Tudor, when it definitively and terribly broke out. Lord Stourton's men attacked Hartgill's home with such success that he had to take refuge in the local church tower. But he fought back, by means of the law, with even greater success. One might have expected that in a local court the peer would win against the commoner, but in fact justice was done: Lord Stourton was declared guilty, ordered to pay damages and committed to the Fleet. At this point what might loosely have been considered fair fight turned ugly and treacherous. On his way to prison Lord Stourton made a detour with the pious explanation that he wanted to pay Hartgill the damages in person. In fact he seized both Hartgill and his son, took them home and murdered them. Justice was again done. Lord Stourton was hanged, presumably with a silken rope, in the market place at Salisbury.

After this, things could hardly go from bad to worse but they stayed bad. After his execution Lord Stourton's estates were forfeit to the crown, which was a ruinous situation enough, but the family now began to suffer the effects of being Catholic. In the reigns of Henry VIII and Edward VI they had shown themselves to be competent though not ignoble trimmers, and naturally under Mary they had come into their own, but on the accession of Elizabeth, after all the martyrdoms and with the Spanish invasion threatening, they were in a weak position indeed.

It went on getting weaker. The 10th Lord Stourton was one of the Catholic peers who were significantly absent from Parliament on the first Guy Fawkes Day and was therefore fined and sent to the Tower. The 11th Lord Stourton was a Royalist and had his house sacked by the Parliamentarians. The 12th, after a series of scares about Popish plots, was, with his co-religionists, excluded from government. The wheel quickened until the 13th Baron followed James II into exile. Not long after, the bankers took over from the barons. In 1717 Henry Hoare started negotiating the purchase of Stourton.

He was the steadiest though not the eldest of the eleven sons of Sir Richard Hoare, a goldsmith banker who had made his name and his way at the time of the Restoration. His name endures, as indeed does his money; he was the founder of Hoare's Bank.

Most of his sons seem to have been a great trial to him. He placed them carefully in various centres of trade abroad, to learn business methods and to gain experience, but found it necessary to cover yards of paper with pints of ink urging them to be better husbands, and he did not mean married men.

Cedars, Stourhead

Stourhead Lake

Carved Bench, Stourhead

*The Bristol Cross and Stourton
Church, Stourhead*

Stourhead

John and James were fairly unsatisfactory but not hopeless. Sir Richard tried to believe that James's 'dizziness proceeded from drinking too much tea and coffee'. But he could have no illusions about Tom. He accepted quite early on, having no alternative, that Tom was disposed to fornication, blasphemy and alcoholism, and other unspecified 'Abominable Wickednesses' (gambling? atheism? homosexuality?) but it took him longer to face the fact that Tom was no businessman and never would be. Poor Tom. He died of consumption in Lisbon ('the Nastiest Citty as ever I saw') a few years before his father died of successful and honourable old age in England.

Henry was presumably a comfort to Sir Richard unless his was the old, old story of the prodigal son's virtuous brother. It seems he was known as 'Good' Henry, perhaps in contrast to Tom, than whom it was all too easy to be better, or perhaps because he supported a number of undoubtedly good causes such as the founding of Westminster Hospital. His tomb describes him as being pious but not censorious. His portrait – fleshy, pursed-mouth – by Dahl makes him look very censorious.

But he built Stourhead. He pulled down Stourton House almost as soon as he had finalised the purchase of the manor in 1720, but not necessarily in a destructive or arrogant spirit; more likely with the realistic view that the building was not only uninhabitable but irreparably so. It was inevitable that what he put in its place would be a Palladian villa. (Sir John Summerson, in *The Classical Country House in 18th-Century England* usefully alerts us to the exact use of the word 'villa'.) Henry Hoare was both cousin and brother-in-law of William Benson, Surveyor General in succession to Sir Christopher Wren. Benson's competence as Surveyor General has sometimes been questioned but never his enthusiasm for the Palladian revival in England. Summerson also cautions us about the word Palladian in this context: 'The initial intention was not so much to celebrate Palladio as Inigo Jones, and the movement was, in its earliest years, quite specifically an Inigo Jones cult.' Certainly in the matter of his own house Benson had put his money where his mouth was by designing Wilbury, Wiltshire, on an Inigo Jones model.

Even without this family pressure, Stourhead would probably have been much as it is, for fashion was running deep and strong in that direction, and rich bankers were among those who liked and needed to be borne along with it. A building boom had started at the beginning of the century: 'All the World are running Mad after Building as far as they can reach,' wrote Vanbrugh to Lord Manchester in 1708. So they were, and so they continued to do: no fewer than fifty houses sprang up between 1720 and 1724. 'Although by no means all the houses built then are Palladian,' explains Summerson, 'it was certainly that boom which carried the style to its long tenure of authority. Conversely it is possible to cite cases where the spirit of Palladianism quickened the desire to build.'

It was equally inevitable that the architect chosen by Hoare would be Colen Campbell, colleague of Benson, influential author of *Vitruvius Britannicus*, the first book on British architecture, and himself as starrily fashionable as the style he advocated and practised. His masterpiece has always been considered to be Wanstead in Essex, designed for the heir of an East India fortune, and largely finished by 1715. It was to become 'a prototype of far-reaching consequence in English architecture' (Summerson) and part of the consequence is Stourhead.

Henry Hoare I – it is more precise than calling him 'Good' – did not live long to enjoy his elegant new house. His soul was not exactly required of him on completion day, but he did die in 1725. Stourhead continued to be a prototype itself, one of the original Palladian villas in England to which architects, builders, land-owners and writers never ceased to refer.

Henry Hoare II could not really exercise much control over Stourhead until his mother died in 1741. Even then, though he was always scrupulous about the maintenance and furnishing of the house, his great contribution was the garden. It was his grandson, Colt Hoare – for his only son died young – who built a greater house than the one he had inherited. He did it in the grand manner, adding a large wing on each side of the original building. The new work cost about £3,500, but it was far from being a mindless gesture of wealth. Colt Hoare was very sensitive about what people thought: 'I am happy it meets with the general approbation of those who see it,' he confided, when the building was well under way. He was probably careful in the selection of those he showed it to, for disobliging remarks *were* made, though presumably out of his hearing.

The most thoughtless layman can see that the sides of the original building were ruined by the extension, yet there is no doubt that the present façade is noble and imposing. At this time of day it is

The Priest's House, Muchelney

almost bound to look pure and right. And it is perceived as a whole, if only because of the practical difficulty of squinting in such a manner as to shut out the accretions and concentrate on the nucleus. In any case the interiors of these two handsome pavilions would be likely to purge any critic of purist objections about their outsides. They are thoroughly handsome rooms, and strangely personal still. The Library has a strong emotional centre to this day, even though the collection which was Colt Hoare's lifework has been dispersed. The Picture Gallery retains the bearing of an apartment that was one of the first of its kind in Europe.

Though Colt Hoare's successors did prodigies of restoration and clearing up after fires, wars and absence, he was the last of the great builders; with one interesting exception: his heir erected a portico which had in fact been intended by Colen Campbell as an essential part of the design.

'I will pull down my barns and build greater.'
'Thou fool, this night thy soul shall be required of thee.'

God does not threaten the greater barns themselves, only the vainglory of their owners. They are not doomed, and may flourish if they are allowed to; and many do. Tintinhull, Lytes Cary and Stourhead, so varied in their positive beauty, have one negative thing in common. They do not look like stranded whales or abandoned hulks, or invite any sad comparisons whatever. Their builders, on the other hand, do provoke melancholy ideas. Here we are, all the visitors and tourists, tramping about and enjoying ourselves, knowing that not one of us probably would have been given house room by the early owners, unless we had respectfully come to mend something. The Almighty may have been overreacting but he did have a point.

Chapter 8

A RUDE LUXURIANCE

THERE ARE few houses open to the public that do not have a famous collection of *something*, and often it is the collection which provides the necessary come-on. Surprisingly, in some cases: apparently the installation of sixteenth- and seventeenth-century portraits from the National Portrait Gallery greatly improved the attendance at Montacute, which one would have thought was an object in itself. Occasionally one meets a collection which might unintentionally act as a deterrent: the alien panelling and fittings gathered from derelict houses are introduced into Barrington Court so arbitrarily that, for example, a staircase, perfectly seemly in itself, suggests a mechanical chair lift for people with weak hearts.

Some of the most enticing collections in Wessex houses are of foreign provenance: Delftware at Dyrham Park; leather wall hangings, almost certainly French, at Dunster Castle. Clevedon Court, Avon, stands out as having two entirely indigenous collections: glass from a nearby town, and pottery which is actually an inside job, the potter being Sir Edmund Harry Elton, 8th Baronet.

'The *colliers* even are more like human beings than the people of the glasshouses,' declared Patty More who knew the glassworks at Nailsea very well. When the glassmaking areas of Bristol were at the height of their prosperity in the eighteenth century, she and her better-known sister Hannah, had founded fifteen Sunday Schools there. In 1791 when Bristol glass had begun to go downhill, no doubt taking the Sunday Schools with it, the two ladies decided to spread their conquests further. In the autumn of that year, 'with a humble reliance on the blessing of Almighty God', they well and truly – that was how they did everything – laid the foundation stone of a Sunday School in Nailsea, nine miles to the south-west of Bristol, and near Clevedon Court where Hannah had a fervent supporter in the Reverend Sir Abraham Elton.

Hannah More gives a wonderful account of the factory. She was shocked when the workers robustly referred to it as Little Hell, for to a fundamentalist Christian leaping flames and punishing heat were no subject for levity. Yet she cannot help making it sound, in some respects, rather nice.

> The work of a glasshouse is an irregular thing, uncertain whether by day or night; not only infringing on man's rest, but constantly intruding upon the Sabbath. The wages high, the eating and drinking luxurious, the body scarcely covered but fed with dainties. The high buildings of the glasshouses ranged before the doors of these cottages – the great furnaces roaring – the swearing, eating and drinking of these half dressed black looking human beings – gave it the most horrible appearance. One if not two joints of finest meat were roasting in each of these hot little kitchens, pots of ale standing about and plenty of early looking vegetables.

All these conditions she must of course have met in Bristol, but both sisters do suggest that at Nailsea there was greater depravity. Patty More is less lyrical on the subject than her sister, and more honest: when Hannah speaks of *talking* to the workers and their families, Patty comes right out with the word 'haranguing'. They were both, however prematurely, Dickensian, and Patty seems prophetically to have faced the fact.

The Nailsea workers may have been worse Christians than their Bristol counterparts but they were much better glassblowers. John Robert Lucas who founded the Nailsea factory in 1788, with the intention of specialising in crown window and bottle glass, had been in the drinks trade, and he may have started his new venture with men who were mere, though skilful, bottlemakers. But as the business grew and prospered he augmented his work force with the very best of the craftsmen who had been laid off by factories in other parts of the country. In the nineteenth century the firm widened its range and perhaps its sophistication by employing a number of French and Belgian craftsmen. They were installed in a row of cottages known as French Rank which has only recently been demolished.

J. R. Lucas was a clever and a decent man. If his portrait is anything to go by, his motto might well have been 'Watch and pray, but particularly watch.' He certainly kept his wits about him:

Barrington Court

Beef Stalls, Barrington Court

when the war with France broke out in 1793 and taxation went sky high; as well as carrying on his regular lines he adapted his window and bottle glass, which carried the lower excise duty, to the production of ware for which it was not normally considered suitable. Apparently no fewer than five excise officers used to keep night-and-day watch on glassmakers, and there was a sixth to see that the other five did not accept bribes, which answers the question 'Quis custodiet ipsos custodes?'

J.R.'s nephew Robert Lucas Chance who took over the Nailsea works in 1810 was an equally astute businessman and as well-judging an opportunist. (I do hope there was a contemporary joke about his middle name being Main.) In 1815, without finally severing his connection with Lucas, Chance and Co., as the Nailsea firm was by this time called, he felt the expediency of developing a glassworks in the Midlands, so this he did, with outstanding success; Chance Bros. Ltd still exists. In the five years that he had spent exclusively at Nailsea his influence had been not only commercial but artistic; without losing any of their vitality the patterns and shapes had become more elegant.

The high reputation of the Nailsea workers has indirectly made life difficult for twentieth-century experts, who have to perform miracles of authentication to establish that a piece in some public or private collection really was made at Nailsea. It is a compliment to those workers that there is such a thing as the Nailsea style and that the expression can be meaningfully used without pedantic reference to either time or place: the style can be found not only in other parts of the country but also a decade before the Nailsea factory was founded.

The 'friggers' are a good example, though only a minor by-product of the Nailsea output. They are the small glass models of objects such as top hats, walking sticks and rolling pins that were made either by apprentices for practice or by fully-trained workers as souvenirs. In both cases they have great charm and show considerable dexterity. The top hats and walking sticks have an Astaire jauntiness. The rolling pins are, inevitably, phallic; and the affectionate inscriptions most of them bear:

> This roller round, it is for you
> If you'll be constant, I'll be true

do suggest that the medium was the message. These friggers

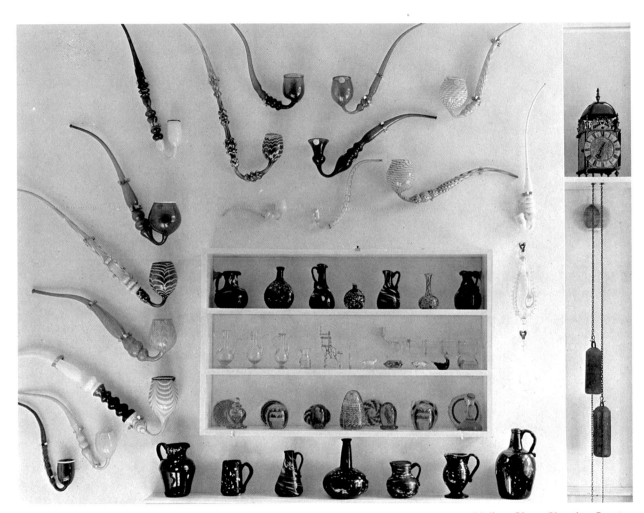

Nailsea Glass, Clevedon Court

Clevedon Court

were usually referred to as Nailsea ware though in fact competent glassblowers all over the country could and did make them.

A sparkling epiphany of Nailsea has gone out all over the world. You come across it in New York, just when you are in quest of something less like home. In England, there is a good display in Taunton County Museum, with some exceptionally pretty pieces such as an elegant pipe in Schiaparelli pink. But the real celebration is undoubtedly at Clevedon Court. A smallish room on the right, just inside the front door, is more or less given over to a dazzling show of items, amassed – affectionately rather than acquisitively, one feels – by the wife of the 9th Baronet.

The show starts quietly, with a case of window glass. Green glass is mysterious and deceptive; if it is blown thin it can look quite colourless but a faint tinge of green somewhere gives it away. More usually, different shades swim about in it like fish. It seems to induce a fluidity of concept in its handlers: it becomes not only a decanter or a flagon but a pair of knitting needles. It meets special-ised needs, and becomes a cucumber trainer or an ear trumpet. These two, by the way, look disturbingly alike; you have to remind yourself that the plant and the sound travel in opposite directions. And like everything else, it can lend itself to perversions: one depressing piece is a witchball, beautiful in itself but lined with scrapbook cutouts, the idea being that this would make it look like porcelain. It does not in the least, but one cannot blame the glassblowers, for the fingers that lined it would have been feminine, engaged in one of the more foolish accomplishments of the time.

In the rest of the display the subtlety of watery green gives way to a forthright prettiness. The glass is boldly coloured: red, brown, blue. The patterns on it – mostly bright white, though a white fleck might have a ravishing pink dot in the centre – are the unmistakable streaks, loops and swirls of Nailsea. One smallish case is sur-mounted by a festoon of glass pipes with wonderfully decorated stems and bowls. Their vitality and grace are startling, yet character-istic.

On the east side of the house, in what used to be a kitchen and where now teas are served, there is further magnificence to look at: rank upon rank of brilliant assertive ceramics, made by Sir Edmund Harry Elton from the 1880s onwards in his Sunflower Pottery only a few yards away across a courtyard.

Sir Edmund Elton is an example to anybody who believes, as I generally do, that amateurs are up to no good and always will be.

His motivation to become a potter seemed poor, in that he knew nothing about pottery and had no reason to suppose he would be any good at it.

His c.v. – if a nineteenth-century baronet had ever had to compile one – would have been disquieting at any stage up to his emergence as a world-famous and highly professional potter. His interests were wide – local government, the fire brigade, landscape painting – but for years the only achievement he could actually point to was the invention of a device for keeping women's skirts out of bicycle wheels. But though he was a Jack of all trades he was master of Clevedon Court from the age of thirty-seven and came of energetic and determined stock.

Looking back in 1910 Sir Edmund gives an engaging account, in *Proceedings of the Somersetshire Archaeological and Natural History Society*, of the beginnings of Elton Ware. He had been thinking for some time, in those early days, about the views of William Morris and his associates on mass production and its effects, and had come to agree with them. But his career as an innovatory potter really began with a visionary experience. He alludes to it, intriguingly, as 'the inspiration which had come upon me in the brick fields'. It happened like this: he was in the local brick fields one day watching the men making tiles, and as he watched an idea came to him with apocalyptic power and suddenness. When he becomes specific about it and we hear that the idea was that he should make 'a sort of mosaic' it seems rather an anticlimax, but in fact it was to supply him with driving-force for the rest of his life.

The particular mosaic which he had in mind to make was a half-length figure of Sir Philip Sidney. The modelling, in three shades of coloured clay, went well enough but then disaster struck, as Sir Edmund frankly relates: 'With the courage born of ignorance I proceeded to the burning, with no better appliance than a disused greenhouse furnace, altered for the purpose according to my crude ideas. The result, as may be expected, was a total failure.'

But from the ashes of Sir Philip Sidney rose Sir Edmund Elton, professional potter. He had had another vision, this time of the horrors of amateurism, and he took steps accordingly. He built a proper kiln using as model a well-tried one he had seen in Bristol; he bought a potter's wheel, and employed a thrower of flower-pots to show him how to use it, after which he practised and practised 'till, in a comparatively short space of time, my desire was obtained, and I could myself produce the shapes required'; he hired a local boy, George Masters, an apprentice who became his 'valued friend and fellow-worker'. Above all he thought out the philosophy of what he was trying to do. Within a year he was producing ware that would sell; not yet to Tiffany but soon.

He attracted useful criticism almost from the first. In 1883 a six-page illustrated article appeared in the *Magazine of Art*. It was by Cosmo Monkhouse, a critic who had been allowed access to Sir Edmund's diary and was therefore accurate about the origins of Elton Ware but who had a lively approach of his own as well. His admiration of the Potter Baronet, as he inevitably came to be known, is based initially on moral grounds. He praises his subject for working by choice when he could have afforded not to. He also admires – and this is very British – his refusal to accept defeat: 'His history is a succession of disasters, but English potters, like English seamen, do not know when they are beaten, and Mr Elton has turned all his mischances into victories.'

This may not seem much of a recommendation nowadays. We all feel we know artists of every kind who should have realised they were beaten long before they did, if indeed they ever did. But Cosmo Monkhouse soon goes on to discuss matters of technique and aesthetics. As a critic he is nothing if not empirical; we see him putting everything to the test: 'From certain very simple experiments I have made with a few fragments of his ware and a hammer, it appears to me to be harder to break, and to be closer in texture than other modern pottery of the same class.' This is a fascinating glimpse. We know how he got hold of the fragments. A paper bag and a trowel would have been enough.

Not long after the First World War the potter W. Fishley Holland went to Clevedon Court to work, having turned down an offer from Bernard Leach. Sir Edmund had died in 1920 (followed soon by George Masters) but as Fishley Holland describes in *Fifty Years a Potter* the master's memory remained 'fresh and unsullied'; in other words, a good many anecdotes and legends were going about. The relevant one in this case is: 'Should any pot have the least blemish, Sir Edmund would throw it against a wall, so there must have been lots of shards until they had gained experience.'

Monkhouse's other experiment, demonstrating the efficiency of the glaze, was even easier. 'You may leave Mr Elton's vases full of water on a bare table without any fear of spoiling the polish.' Another fascinating glimpse.

Throughout the article, Monkhouse insists on Elton's great originality, but without absolutely defining it. It is when he comes to the decoration of the ware that he is most explicit, both in scattered comments ('Mr Elton is rather fond of snakes') and sustained paragraphs.

> Mr Elton is almost an Oriental. He is also one in his gift of what is called conventionalising natural forms. Yet he is thoroughly modern and English withal, taking his suggestions from the flowers and animals he knows, and treating them with a freedom which is only limited by his personal taste. I am afraid that neither his fauna nor his flora have an exact counterpart in the world of nature; but they are admirably suited to the artificial world of decoration.

Obviously Cosmo Monkhouse could at that time speak only of the early Elton products, which were essentially slip-ware. Sir Edmund gives 1902 as the date when he made a new departure by introducing gold into his decoration. He had been in two minds about it because of 'the vulgarity so easily introduced with gold', but like most inventors he solved the problem by accident, as with characteristic frankness he explains: 'One day I noticed a curious appearance, where some gold overlapped the platinum.' This resulted in crackle-ware, the secret of which was the imposing of gold on other precious metals. It is lovely but fortunately it never completely ousted his first style.

Elton Ware has to be seen to be believed. It is weirdly eclectic. The forms hark back to almost everything that ever had a distinctive shape, and they sometimes alter on the way up as though the wheel changed its mind. A vase may start off as burly and commodious as a cache-pot but end with a nipped-in neck into which no flower-pot could possibly be inserted. The usage they suggest is complex too. The bottom half of a jug may seem meant for some gracious domestic fluid – oil or milk or wine – but the only liquid which could fittingly be poured from the terrible dragon's face which forms the lip would be strong poison, and the only hand which could grasp the dragon's comb that forms the handle would be not that of the lady of the house but of some very large thug.

There is a splendid theatricality about every piece. (No doubt the boring ones ended up against the wall with the flawed ones.) A large three-handled drinking vessel, on the lines of a posset pot and with a surface of gold crazy paving, hints at some well-endowed pageant or some production of *Henry IV Part II* where money was no object.

The colours – blue, green, pink, brown, mauve – are Islamic in their brightness, and the glaze can make them quite blinding. But they lack Islamic discipline and coherence; they slip and swirl and tangle with each other in a brilliant disorder that is too exotic to be called marbling. The decoration, however, is done with a very firm hand. An incisive pink butterfly is raised neatly above the welter, and a garland of fruit and flowers is clamped as hard and fast as a pair of handcuffs round an indeterminate eddy of colours.

A word about the snakes, since Monkhouse points out that Elton was rather fond of them. Their expressions suggest that this was reciprocal. They are an amiable lot on the whole. One of them spirals up the neck of a blue-green vase, then turns its head out into the room, with no menace but as if about to give a diffident cough.

Si monumentum requiris, you will find one in the town: a splendid clock tower which Elton made and installed in honour of Queen Victoria's Jubilee. It is rich with mosaics of birds, flowers and fruit, and expressive with a ceramic portrait of Father Time. Two other pieces by Elton which are almost grand enough to be thought of as monuments are at present in the Chapel: a pair of candlesticks which have both stature and authority. Apart from the display in the house, there are some good show-cases in Taunton County Museum.

In speaking of Elton Ware, Cosmo Monkhouse uses the catchy phrase 'a rude luxuriance'. The tone of the article is such that there can be nothing unflattering about the adjective; it cannot suggest 'unskilled' or 'barbarous' or 'harsh'. I looked in the *OED* for some other, more accurate meaning, and found it: 'vigorous'. This is a word which applies not only to Elton ceramics but to much of Nailsea glass, so the description can embrace them both: a rude luxuriance.

Chapter 9

MEN OF DORSET

Whether the monks of the Benedictine Abbey of Cerne traced his
outlines, or whether, as legends declare, this was a work of the early
pagan Saxons, and intended by them to represent their God, Heil,
to whom human sacrifices were offered here, *must ever be matters
for conjecture*. (Italics mine)

THE CLOUD of unknowing which hangs low over the Cerne Giant
was obviously felt by C. G. Harper to be appropriate: a kind of
bloom best left untouched. His anxiety not to commit himself to
any particular conjecture left him with one rather weak hypothesis.
I really cannot imagine the good Benedictines tracing the giant's
outlines in so public a place, unless Mr Harper means outlines as
opposed to details.

The giant's phallus is so assertive, and the style of C. G. Harper,
an essentially Victorian writer, so well-bred, that it is rather surprising he should draw attention to the figure at all. The explanation
may be that at the beginning of the century the giant had been
neglected and that his impropriety was therefore veiled by grass.
Certainly at that period, as Mr Harper robustly admits, Cerne
Abbas was in such a depressed state it seems unlikely that any of
its inhabitants would go out cleaning up a giant on the hillside: 'If
you would make acquaintance with a dead town, allow me to
introduce you to Cerne Abbas. It is a weary, age-worn place, a little
off the main road, and rapidly falling into decay.'

Yet cleaning up is what the giant seems frequently to have
needed and indeed received. Ralph Wightman in *Portrait of Dorset*
(1965) believes he would have vanished altogether if left alone for
much more than a hundred years. A logical extension of his belief

is that the Benedictines, in the course of their long local reign, must have been the ones who carried out, instigated or at least sanctioned the scouring of his white trenches and the trimming of his grass. Wightman does not for a moment suggest that they were responsible for the original carving, nor that they approved of or recommend it, but he sensibly points out that with the authority they wielded they could have let it go to ruin if they had wished. They were obviously conservationists. It was an attitude that was ecumenically held by Anglicans too at a later age. In the eighteenth century the churchwardens and some of the parishioners used to lend a hand with the work of maintenance. However little is known about the Cerne Giant it is clear that he was popular.

He had his uses. For centuries he was a scapegoat, held responsible not only for unorthodox pregnancies but for the mass deflowerings that took place on his hillside in the course of May Day celebrations. He was also a convenient bogeyman. In *The Dynasts* Hardy shows his fellow countrymen using the giant as a metaphor when they wish to make a conclusive point about the awfulness of Napoleon, himself a bogeyman.

> I can tell you a word or two on't. It is about his victuals. They say that he lives upon human flesh, and has rashers of baby every morning for breakfast – for all the world like the Cernel Giant in old ancient times.

He has often provided an opportunity for moral indignation. His first appearance in print was honourable: a clear and uncensored drawing in the *Gentleman's Magazine* of 1764. Ten years later, however, the *Dorset County History* depicted him without his phallus. Seeing it measures thirty feet, as much as a sixth of his height, this bid for propriety simply leaves a suggestive gap. Victorian drawings and descriptions for the most part omitted it too; writers who felt they could not make such a clean sweep tended to allude to 'indications of the phallic corruptions to which the worship of the all-vivifying sun invariably led'. Our own permissive age has produced some stern letters suggesting that the giant should wear a loin-cloth or have his head and feet re-shaped so that he is facing into the hill.

Quite the best account of the Cerne Giant is to be found in a special issue of the *Dorset County Magazine*, which appeared recently. Most of it is written by Rodney Legg, editor of the magazine,

The Cerne Giant

whose editorial is a plea to us, the sixty-sixth generation of those who have known and tended the giant, to remember that our duty is to pass him on intact to the sixty-seventh generation. The idea of being responsible for the survival of the Cerne Giant is persuasive in itself, but Mr Legg supports his appeal with some exhilarating arguments.

The giant has usually been listed as Romano-British and his date guessed to be AD 191, this being a year when Commodus was Emperor. Certainly the giant brandishes a club in the attitude of Hercules, a reincarnation of whom Commodus declared himself to be. But one club is much the same as another, and one club-brandisher too, in any age or environment, and Mr Legg supports a theory put forward by several scholars recently that the giant is not Romano-British at all but British, that he was made a century and a half earlier, by the Durotriges, the Celtic tribe that lived in Dorset, and that specifically he was the god Nodons. This would make him a contemporary of the Uffington White Horse.

I need hardly say that viable evidence is given for each step of this theory but, instead of paraphrasing all of it, I should like to quote one point. It has frequently been suggested that the white horse originally had a rider who has since been effaced or just grassed over: and furthermore that the rider was not a man but a phallus. One could argue of course that one phallus is much like another, but this does seem to bring the giant and the horse very close together. Mr Legg reminds us of one of our most respectable nursery rhymes – if indeed any of them is:

Ride a cock horse to Banbury Cross
To see a fine lady upon a white horse.

I am convinced.

For the best view of the Cerne Giant today, most guide books recommend the lay-by on the A352, and if not the best it is certainly the closest; yet far enough away, for on the hill itself all you see is the flowing white line of a heel or the scalloped ridge of fingertips, isolated in the grass. From the air he seems too prostrate for his character, and the rectangular enclosure which now surrounds him – it used to be hexagonal – makes him look as though he is being offered up on a tray.

I much prefer to either of these the view from Cow Down Hill on the road leading out of Sydling St Nicholas. It was here at the beginning of the descent into Cerne Abbas that I first sighted him on a Sunday morning of mist and sun in early February. It was a fair distance across the valley and I was using field glasses. Some elderly churchgoers driving past gave me an odd look but it was well worth it. The glasses cut him away from his hill and even with his feet turned sideways he seemed to be striding forward out of the turf and through the haze.

In this landscape, with the chalk staring through the grass in a way red earth could never do, something like a man or a beast seems to be lurking in every field and on every hillside ready to jump out. The giant is part of his environment that has got away. The other men of Dorset that I have chosen give a similar impression of being embodiments of their countryside. They have something else in common with each other and with the giant: a great manliness, or perhaps, as this word is currently in disrepute, I should say personality.

Lime Kiln Hill, West Bexington

The Tolpuddle Martyrs (who, if it had not been for the wave of gentility that swept down the River Piddle in the nineteenth century like a bore, would have been the Tolpiddle Martyrs) come to life on a village green under a spreading tree. Even though nowadays it is called the Martyrs' Tree, and a seat with a thatched shelter has been erected in their honour, and traffic bellows past with no pause or rhythm, it is easy to imagine them standing there, with others, exchanging the first words of a dialogue that was to lead them in chains to a different community on the other side of the world.

They were George Loveless, James Loveless (his brother), James Hammett, Thomas Standfield, John Standfield (his son), and James Brine. Thomas Standfield, at forty-four, was the oldest and James Brine, at twenty, the youngest. The official contemporary portrait of five of them which appeared in Cleave's *Penny Gazette of Variety* shows them in neat stiff clothes with their hair scrupulously combed and parted, and charnel-house expressions. Sunday clothes and sedate bearing they could certainly have assumed when necessary, for five of them were Methodists and two lay preachers, but it is easier to see them under the tree in the labourers' clothes so familiar from woodcuts in social history books: open-necked shirts, loose waistcoats, baggy trousers with leggings, and broad-brimmed hats.

In those days, the eighteen-thirties, their diet would have been low and their cottages small, but they were decidedly not the potato-eating, tea-drinking underlings described by Cobbett earlier in the century, nor did they correspond to William Howitt's definition of a farm labourer in *The Rural Life of England* (1838): 'He is as much of an animal as air and exercise, strong living and sound sleeping can make him, and he is nothing more.'

They were thoughtful men, and highly articulate; as religious nonconformists they would have taken a healthy pleasure in the sound of their own voices. And they had a very real grievance. When George Loveless, the leader of the group, said in his own defence, 'We were uniting to preserve ourselves, our wives and our children from utter degradation and starvation,' he was speaking the simple truth. At that time the average weekly wage for farm labourers in Dorset was ten shillings. With good luck and economy a family could just live on this sum. But in Tolpuddle in the course of only a few years it went down to nine shillings, to eight, to seven, and there was even talk of its going down to six shillings. It was at this point that the men acted.

George Loveless was also speaking the simple truth when he declared: 'We have injured no man's reputation, character, person or property.' They had not; there had been no verbal or physical abuse, no rick-burning, no wrecking of machines. They had tried peaceful persuasion. The vicar had helped them to organize an appeal to local landowners and farmers from whom they received the most generous promises that there should be a minimum weekly wage of ten shillings. But none of these promises was implemented.

In the autumn of 1833 the men turned for advice to the Grand National Consolidated Trades Union, founded earlier in the year by Robert Owen, and two delegates came down to Tolpuddle. The result of their visit was the setting up of the Tolpuddle Grand Lodge of Agricultural Labourers Friendly Society. This kind of activity was perfectly legal in itself and had been for ten years, but it must have frightened the Dorset magistrates (trade unionism in Tolpuddle) for on February 22, 1834 Loveless and his friends were arrested, their crime being the taking of unlawful oaths.

These dreadful oaths were no more than the pledges of loyalty which they had made at an initiation ceremony, as it was darkly described, at Thomas Standfield's cottage on December 9, two and a half months before. Unfortunately for the six men the Unlawful Oaths Act of 1797, passed in order to deal with a specific naval mutiny, had never been repealed, and by a malicious stretch of imagination and logic was held to apply to the farm labourers.

Hardy Monument

*From Whitenothe Cliff towards
Portland Bill*

Neither reminder nor warning of this obscure and inappropriate act was given until four days before the arrest.

In the circumstances nobody was surprised when the six men were found guilty but many of those present in the Dorchester courtroom were horrified by the severity of the sentence: seven years' transportation.

The evening before the sailing of the convict ship George Loveless wrote to his wife:

> Depend upon it, it will work together for good and we shall yet rejoice together. I hope you will pay particular attention to the morals and spiritual interest of the children. Don't send me any money to distress yourself. I shall do well, for He who is Lord of the winds and waves will be my support in life and death.

Against all probability his courage and faith were justified. The mental and bodily sufferings of the six men while abroad were almost beyond what they could bear. But at home a widespread agitation for their release provoked mass meetings, vast demonstrations, relentless questions in Parliament and petitions with nearly a million signatures; and finally led, in 1836, to a full and free pardon. Communications and travel being so inadequate it was months before the men actually got back; but George and Betsy Loveless did at last rejoice together.

The men and their families prospered into old age, especially the five who eventually emigrated to Canada and became farmers. James Hammett settled in Tolpuddle once more, but as a builder not as a farm labourer. The village remembers them all. There is a memorial arch at the Methodist chapel. There is the memorial seat under the Martyrs' Tree: a celebration of the hundredth anniversary of the trial. Also in 1934 six cottages were built, each bearing the name of one of the martyrs, by the TUC, who at the same time honoured James Hammett's grave in the churchyard with a tombstone, handsomely carved by Eric Gill and bearing a title which, unlike most appellations, only six men in the world have any right to: TOLPUDDLE MARTYR.

The monument that stands, with misplaced confidence, on Blackdown ridge looking out over Chesil Bank to Lyme Bay and the Channel with Portland Bill to the east celebrates yet another man of Dorset: Vice-Admiral Sir Thomas Masterman Hardy, flag-captain of the *Victory* at the Battle of Trafalgar. I describe him like this for two reasons. The first is that the monument is often thought to commemorate Thomas Hardy the novelist. This is silly, as the octagonal stone tower which was designed by Arthur Dyke Acland-Troyte and built in 1844, when the novelist was four years old, is what Pevsner calls 'that Victorian thing, a monument' and is unmistakably of its time with its crinoline base and busty top, and air of take-it-or-leave-it grandeur. Hardy the novelist lived until 1928 and got Eric Kennington.

The two men were in fact distantly related. The le Hardy family had come over from Jersey in the sixteenth century and settled in Dorset. At one time the novelist seriously thought of calling himself le Hardy as sounding more distinguished (*Jude the Obscure* by Thomas le Hardy); it apparently never crossed the mind of the sailor. He came from a family of yeomen who knew their place and quite liked it. The girls married well-to-do farmers and country lawyers. The eldest sons farmed; younger ones went to sea.

The second reason is that Hardy's presence at Nelson's deathbed is the only thing most people seem to know about him. It is as if he was born simply in order to stand in the shadowy blood-stained cockpit feeling as much grief and anxiety as he had time for with the noise of battle going on outside, and to utter certain words. Thomas Hardy the poet would have thought of the occasion precisely in these terms: the Spinner of the Years would have said, 'Now,' Nelson would have said, 'Kiss me, Hardy,' and Hardy would have kissed him. In fact Hardy lived and actively pursued his career for another thirty-four years.

Whereas the famous Devon sailors of an earlier age had all been more or less pirates, Hardy was a great sailor after the Dorset fashion, equally brave and resourceful but well within the system. He was a thorough professional. Even in his own lifetime and not just to distinguish him from the other Thomas Hardy he was referred to as Nelson's Hardy. Many people would feel diminished by being anybody's somebody, but Hardy seems to have moved in a world where such considerations were irrelevant.

The story goes – it would – that from early childhood he had wanted to go to sea. He certainly acquired few of the skills usually learnt in youth such as literacy. In 1782 when he was thirteen he wrote to his brother: 'The close Mr Bagter sent are to large but they do prety well.' It is always tempting to blame the teachers, but in fact Crewkerne Grammar School had a very good record. Life did nothing for his spelling and syntax. After the attack on Copenhagen in 1801 he describes how he and Nelson went on shore.

His lordship and myself was on shore yesterday, when,
extraordinary to be told, he was received with as much acclamation
as when we went to Lord Mare's Show.

Yet his seamanship, since he first joined the brig *Helena* in 1781,
seems never to have been in question.

It was in 1793 when he was promoted lieutenant and posted to
the frigate *Meleager*, after a sound training in many types of craft,
that he first came in contact with Nelson to whose squadron, then
in the Mediterranean, the frigate was attached. It was more than
two years before he really caught Nelson's eye, but when he did it
was in no uncertain fashion. The ship that brought him luck in this
respect was the French prize *Minerve* to which he and the captain
of the *Meleager* were transferred. On at least three occasions his
courage and skill in handling the *ci-devant* French frigate either
saved her from defeat or helped her to victory, as at the Battle of
Cape St Vincent. And Nelson was watching.

He was impressed, as a wonderful *Boy's Own* anecdote describes.
One day off Gibraltar Hardy had put out a boat to rescue a man
who had fallen overboard in the very path of a hostile Spanish
fleet. A current caught the boat and carried it towards the
Spaniards. Nelson seeing the danger called out: 'By God, I'll not
lose Hardy. Back the mizzen topsail.' I suppose we all have a
fantasy that one day somebody important will say that by God
they'll not lose us and back the mizzen topsail, but it really happened to Hardy.

In his honoured old age and possibly his cups, when he was
Governor of Greenwich Hospital, Hardy told a number of stories
the climax of which was something Lord Nelson had been heard
to say about him. One of these utterances was 'Tom Hardy shall
be my Captain one of these days'. Another fantasy perhaps, but
the point is that whether Nelson said it or not, he did it. After the
Battle of the Nile he asked Hardy to be his flag-captain on the
Vanguard. In 1803 he insisted on his being flag-captain of the *Victory*.

The two men were as close as mutual respect and trust could
make them. Hardy had one or two bees in his bonnet, and the
queen bee was Lady Hamilton. He felt that Nelson was making a
complete fool of himself over her. Many people thought it at the
time and many others have thought it since, but Hardy acted on
the idea. Once when a boat's crew appealed to Lady Hamilton to
get them out of trouble, Hardy not only flogged them for the

offence but added another twelve lashes for their having asked Lady Hamilton to intercede in the first place; and then told her what he had done. However the confidence between Nelson and Hardy survived even this incident.

As a result of Trafalgar Hardy was made a baronet and soon after – it was a hereditary title – decided to marry. Louisa Hardy was a snob; she never tried to forget that she had been born a *Berkeley* and consistently treated the Hardys with contempt. She was a flirt; on one occasion when Hardy got back to London he had to fight a duel. Fortunately, for posterity, she was also a chatterbox; almost from the time she learned to write until the day she could no longer hold a pen she chattered away to her diary. A great many extracts from these volumes can be found in John Gore's *Nelson's Hardy and his Wife* (1935). (A good title: Hardy belonged to Nelson but Louisa belonged to him.)

Lady Hardy wrote without selection or insight but, as at the first opportunity she threw herself into Society, she cannot help being interesting. She knew everybody, or thought she did. When the time came she devoted her best energies to finding eligible husbands for her three pretty daughters, but with surprisingly little success. Her real coup was in finding a second husband for herself: Lord Seaford, who waited gallantly in the wings for years until death closed Sir Thomas's honourable career.

The Hardy marriage may well have been a happy enough partnership in its way but a close relationship it cannot have been, for the Admiral was away sometimes for as long as three years at a stretch. He wrote infrequently and his wife's chatter was not often directed his way.

Presumably there should be a statue on top of the Hardy monument; the platform is there and the tower looks odd and truncated without a figure. It must have been easy to get a likeness of Hardy. When one comes across his portrait – in the Dorset County Museum, for example – whatever the pose his face looks exactly the same: big-boned, well-fed, handsome and resolute, with a very sensuous mouth. He would have looked well on the monument, looking out to sea, as ready to stride away from his hill as the Cerne Giant. The impression is so strong that the tower, even without him, seems to be turning its back on the fields and heath and woods inland.

Brean Down

Chapter 10

HIGH AND LOW

Eternal mists their dropping curse distil
And drizzly vapours all the ditches fill.
The swampy land's a bog, the fields are seas
And too much moisture is the grand disease.
Here every eye with brackish rheum o'erflows
And a fresh drop still hangs at every nose.

THIS cry from the heart was sent up at Brent Knoll, Somerset, in a poem by William Diaper, its curate for two years at the beginning of the eighteenth century. (Wessex clergymen through the ages have tended to have names like Bastard, Bottome and Diaper.) Today Brent Knoll is regarded by most of us as a shapely and useful landmark that tells us where we have got to on the M5, even if we do not need the Rest Area to which it has given its name. Except for occasional buffeting, there is nothing to grumble about on the drive through the flat green country north of Taunton with its distant views of the surrounding ranges of hills: the Blackdowns, the Quantocks and the Mendips.

In any case it is well known that clergymen, especially when poets as well, have an unedifying history of moaning about their parishes, not the souls so much as the scenery. In some cases they had their reasons; Hawker of Morwenstow certainly did and they were a credit to him. But Herrick of Dean Prior was the incumbent of one of the prettiest, healthiest livings in the country. So it is difficult to take the Reverend William Diaper's moans seriously; until one starts climbing.

From any of the tors, mumps, downs and knolls which were once thrown up out of the Somerset plain it is easy to see what the trouble was. From higher up, the view is too romantic: in *Highways and Byways of Somerset* Edward Hutton described how north-west of Wells the traveller (himself in 1912) looking south 'will see spread out beneath him a vast and mysterious plain, blue and grey and gold in the setting sun'. He, however, was not only a native returning, and from a long stay in Italy at that, but he was standing on top of the Mendips at the time. If he had been standing on Brent Knoll his vision might have been different.

Brent Knoll is 550 feet, high enough to look imposing on a wet plain but not too high to show that the plain is very wet indeed, even today. It has been much worse of course. Brent Knoll was once an island. At various times and in various ways people have tried to do something about it.

There is some evidence that it was the Romans who first attempted to dry out the wetlands of Somerset. It would have been characteristic; not only were they good engineers but they rose to challenges of this kind. Archaeologists have discovered the remains of sea-walls and embankments all along the coastal clay belt, which includes Brent Knoll, and have suggested that some of them may have been the work of the Romans.

Medieval reclamation concentrated more on inland areas and used other methods such as the alteration of the courses of rivers, the provision of a system of drainage ditches, known as rhynes, and the construction of causeways which not only carried roads to the islands but helped to control the floods. Glastonbury Abbey inspired and organized much of this work, but a dispute arose with the dignitaries of Wells Cathedral who had a rival claim to the lands which were being made viable. For a time the parties concerned put a great deal of valuable energy into such activities as setting fire to each other's barns and destroying each other's piggeries, for the greater glory of God.

By the end of the Middle Ages, though much had been achieved in the way of reclamation, the impetus had been temporarily lost. The sixteenth century did not completely ignore the problem, and when at the beginning of the seventeenth century there was a great flood in Somerset, and Glastonbury Tor became an island again, the necessary stimulus to further progress seemed to have been provided, but though successively James I, Charles I and Cromwell discussed proposals for drainage, nothing came of any of them; worse than nothing in Cromwell's case for he turned down the services of Cornelius Vermuyden.

It was not until the end of the eighteenth century that the work really went forward again, and became more comprehensive, the chief measure being the digging of a new channel for the River Cary: the King's Sedgemoor Drain. By the middle of the nineteenth century the wetlands of Somerset were declared to be drained, though in fact the problem of flooding was not thoroughly brought under control until after the Second World War.

So, to return to the Reverend William Diaper at Brent Knoll: it was not surprising that at the beginning of the eighteenth century he regarded his environment with such despair. In the poem already cited (it was a long one), he lamented his isolation:

> Sure this is nature's gaol for rogues designed.
> Whoever lives in Brent must live confined.
> Moated around, the water is our fence.
> None comes to us, and none can go from hence.

He was no doubt exaggerating, but there must have been a great deal in what he said. It is ironical that the motorway should now come so close. It would have given him grievances of another kind.

Brean Down is now a headland, the last but one appearance of the Mendips. (The very last visible coil of the monster's tail is Steep Holm, well out into the Bristol Channel.) It is nearly 300 feet high and overlooks – to an extent shelters – Weston-super-Mare. As it is only a few miles north of Brent Knoll what Diaper says of his immediate district applies here too.

> We are to north and southern blasts exposed
> Still drowned by one or by the other frozen.

I can vouch for the truth of this statement, and indeed would go further. The afternoon we were on Brean Down we drowned *and* frozen. It is a melancholy place, especially in late autumn when the lighthouse on Flat Holm, off the Welsh coast, starts blinking and the Channel turns from pewter to charcoal, and the mists start crawling about over Sedgemoor.

Brean Down and Brent Knoll have much in common as well as the wind and the rain: an Iron Age fort, the remains or traces of a temple, signs of a field system and evidence of occupation from Beaker times. The headland also has a much later fortification, manned successfully against Napoleon III, the Kaiser and Hitler, though in the event none of them came.

Brean Down must have seemed more obstinately an island than

Brent Knoll in the days when the Romans were building sea walls, for on its north side it had to contend with the estuary of the Axe, a traditionally wilful river. From the coarse grass top of the headland it is easy to see that it is a peninsula still and to imagine how the thrashing waves of the Channel beat their way right round it, not so much separating it from the other island hills in this dingy shallow sea as joining them to it; they were all in it together.

There was little solidarity, however. For centuries the contact between these hills and between them and the mainland must for most people have been entirely visual. Until the Middle Ages the only means of closer communication would have been by boat, and probably such dreary voyaging was never undertaken except by traders and troublemakers. We are told that the Iron Age hill-fort dwellers were an aggressive and suspicious people who lived in terms of tribal quarrels and strictly local interests, unable to see, as the Romans did, how the British could become an integrated nation. Brent Knoll seen from Brean Down looks watchful and protective, a reliable sentinel, reassuring to have there, but the reality seems to have been very different.

The most heroic of the troublemakers, one who did journey from island to island, was King Alfred. His hideout was Athelney. It was there he took refuge before fighting and winning the campaign against the Danes in 878. Contemporary writers emphasise that the island was extremely difficult to find. It still is, now that the water has gone, being only about thirty feet above sea level.

From Burrow Mump

The most famous of the traders were Joseph of Arimathea and the young Jesus, even if they were never there. The legend has always been so prevalent that it begins to be persuasive, though Joseph himself was sighted so often and in so many places that he was almost too ubiquitous for belief. I can see them sitting upright in the boat looking around them with beady eyes, the tough successful trader, already planning to invest in a really handsome tomb, and his likely apprentice, being rowed across England's grey and unpleasant waters to Glastonbury.

The best view of Sedgemoor is from Burrow Mump which rises out of the plain with such startling abruptness that some say it must be the work of man, though anyone who knows Wessex will recognize the work of nature. There was once a small Norman castle on top, which has been superseded by a curious amalgam of the ruins of a medieval chapel and parts of an eighteenth-century church. On the outside of the tower there is a memorial tablet to

Burrow Mump

the men and women of Somerset who died in the Second World War. It is very touching, in that place with the whole of Somerset so visibly and beautifully around it.

The best time for the view is after prolonged and heavy rainfall, but the traveller will not have to wait long for these conditions; the surrounding hills are notorious. When the sun comes out, however coldly, after days of rain, the effect is dazzling. Pre-drainage writers so often described the waters of Sedgemoor as murky that it must have been more than a cliché. The water that is left, in ditches and drains and well-regulated rivers (the Parrett and the Tone run near Burrow Mump), is wincingly bright.

The land is mostly pasture these days. There used to be large crops of withy and teazle but, now that plastic is in and velvet is out, there is less call for them. The straight ditches round the shining green fields, often fringed with willows, enclose black-and-white cattle. The other day about twenty bullocks were running really fast round their meadow as though a warble-fly was after them, but as the recent warble-fly plague is now deemed to be over, and as the bullocks were moving cheerfully, it must have been some celebration gallop. It was a pleasant sight.

Burrow Mump is near Athelney and not far west of the village of Othery. In the distance, directly to the north, stands a very fine church tower, that of Weston Zoyland. It was in this parish that the battle of Sedgemoor was fought, on July 6, 1685. When it was all over, five hundred rebel soldiers lay imprisoned in the church, groaning and speculating below the magnificent angels on the roof of the nave. Some of them died of their wounds and the rest were in such a sad state that, according to the Churchwardens' Accounts Book, five shillings and eight pence were spent on the burning of frankincense, saltpetre and resin 'after ye prisoners were gone out'; mostly to a horrible death as other church records, complete with gruesome illustrations, attest. On July 8 eight shillings and eight pence were paid to the ringers when Monmouth was caught, having nearly got to Poole Harbour.

The whole campaign is full of mysteries, the most interesting being why anyone, royalist or rebel, should risk a battle on Sedgemoor, given the nature of the terrain at that period. The Duke of Monmouth landed, quite sensibly, at Lyme Regis on June 11 and then seems to have spent nearly a month wandering about Dorset and Somerset without pressing his initial advantage. (It is easy to criticise, and no doubt any historian could make it seem perfectly natural.) He had to rally troops, of course, and proclaim himself King (which he did at Taunton) before he marched towards London. This, in fact, he had begun to do when the Royal Army arrived in Bristol. He then retreated to Bridgwater where he had already been once.

In the end he marched straight into trouble. On July 15 the Royal Army camped at Weston Zoyland. Monmouth heard of this and decided to attack them at night. The Rebel Army set out from Bridgwater at eleven in the evening – these last hours are well documented – and arrived in the neighbourhood just after midnight, predictably in a thick mist. The guide, though a local man from Chedzoy, took them down the wrong lane, which again was fairly foreseeable in those conditions. They were spotted, the alarm was given and the battle began. Watchers on Burrow Mump (the noise might well have attracted the inhabitants of Burrow Bridge and perhaps Othery as well to such a vantage point) would have seen the lights of torches, lanterns and gunfire moving in a deadly tangle. Just before dawn Monmouth fled from the field.

The monument on the battlefield, put up in 1928, states that it is in memory of all those who fell in the battle of Sedgemoor, 'doing the right as they saw it'. These liberal sentiments, though acceptable to modern ears, are so emphatically *not* how Judge Jeffreys saw it that they almost add insult to injury.

Glastonbury Tor is the most spectacular of the isolated hills of Somerset, partly because it rises not from a plain but from a ridge. Yet it is far from being the most sympathetic. It suffers from a plague of conflicting and mindless legends and superstitions and because of this has become a resort for the tender-minded.

The authors of *The Archaeology of Somerset*, Michael Aston and Ian Burrow (such a good name for an archaeologist), point out that a site like Glastonbury can never be appreciated as long as people ask such questions as 'Was this Arthur's stronghold?' and 'Is this an early monastery?' The second question in fact is not very dangerous as the Faith is tough and continuous but the first question is lethal. The only questions that get anybody anywhere according to Aston and Burrow (with whom I agree) are: 'Was this site an economic centre?', 'How big an area was dependent on it?', 'What resources were available to it?'

The various branches of alternative archaeology, as it is politely called, which draw wide-eyed crowds to places like Glastonbury, are discussed by Richard Muir in *Prehistoric and Roman Britain*.

Glastonbury Tor

Of the findings of astro-archaeology he mildly comments that 'prehistorians have often been nonplussed and surprised to be told that the technologically unsophisticated people that they had studied for years and thought they knew were really ace astronomers and top-notch mathematicians'.

As Dr Muir warms to his theme he gets, I am glad to say, quite violent.

Unfortunately, the astronomical propositions tend often to be absorbed into the rag-bag of nonsensical ideas, mumbo-jumbo and witch cults which constitute 'alternative archaeology'. The alternatives on offer amount to no more of an alternative to patient, scholarly study and painstaking excavation and interpretation than jumping off the top of Glastonbury Tor is an alternative to space flight.

His demolition of leylines is masterly.

The 'leyline' case, which suggests that the prehistoric countryside was traversed by straight trackways linking up all manner of monuments, is no case at all. Its only remarkable feature is the inability of its proponents to offer any leylines which are even remotely interesting or provocative. Most of the lines are propped up by relatively young churches with well-recorded histories, Scots pine trees planted in the eighteenth century or later, ponds of interest only to thirsty cows, rather boring little stones and straight tracks provided not by Stone Age mystics but by the Parliamentary Enclosure commissioners of the eighteenth and nineteenth centuries. The leylines often manage to miss their supposed targets by a good many yards and studiously avoid a multitude of monuments known to real archaeologists.

Much more will be discovered about Glastonbury Tor than is at present known but, as the archaeologists point out, any sound evidence of anything at all is bound to cause distress to those who cannot welcome the passing of a mystery to which only they hold the key. But Glastonbury Tor will always be beautiful and majestic, always a heart-warming sign of home to men and women of Somerset, even if the truth about it should be unpalatable. And, though some of the present myths are irritating, most are at least cheerful. The idea of resurrection runs strongly through them. Joseph of Arimathea's thorn will blossom every year. Arthur is sleeping but one day he will rise from his tomb to lead us all.

Christ will come again in glory; *somewhere* between Land's End and Glastonbury Tor.

Across the county border, in the chalk uplands of Wiltshire, rises a hill of a different shape, not a cone but a wide, gentle bulge, lower than it used to be because so much soil has washed down, but never very high: Windmill Hill. It must have asserted itself first of all by its extent: the outermost of the three concentric circles is 1,200 feet across; and later by its seniority – it is at least six centuries older than the Avebury circle which lies in the valley below – until its very seniority put it at a disadvantage beside newcomers who used bronze rather than stone.

Writers through the ages have praised Windmill Hill's grass, the plumpness of the sheep who ate it, and the fragrance of its air, but it is by no means the resort that these compliments imply. It has great authority and indeed it is an archetype, for as a causewayed camp it gave its name to the earliest Neolithic culture in Britain. In the evening it suggests mortality rather than convalescence.

Men and women lived there before the first pyramids were built, and were buried nearby – the important ones, that is – in West Kennett Long Barrow. But the site had many uses. From the bones found there it is clear that it was also a corral-cum-abattoir into which the autumn cattle were rounded up and if necessary slaughtered.

From high to low everything is at the mercy of the weather and the seasons. Louis MacNeice in his poem 'Wessex Guidebook' put it precisely:

> those illiterate seasons
> Still smoke their pipes in swallow-hole and hide-out
> As scornful of the tractor and the jet
> As of the Roman road, or axe of flint,
> Forgotten by the mass of human beings
> Whom they, the seasons, need not even forget
> Since, though they fostered man, they never loved him.

Wells Tor

Stonehenge Down

Windmill Hill

Avebury Stone Circle and Village

Avebury and the Great Barn

Little Solsbury Hill, Bath

Win Green Hill, near
Shaftesbury

White Horse, Cherhill Down

Chapter 11

RETURNED THROUGH THE WOOD

COLERIDGE MOVED to Nether Stowey at the end of 1796 and settled with his wife, to whom he had been married for just over a year, and his baby son Hartley, in a cottage found for him by Thomas Poole.

For Coleridge, Thomas Poole was a mixture of muse, impresario and house agent, and he was clearly a bustler in general. On the tombstone in Nether Stowey churchyard, above the grave where he and his parents lie buried, he is simply 'Son of the Above', but the memorial tablet inside the church is overcrowded with his virtues. Some are vague but predictable: he was distinguished 'for integrity of life and inestimable qualities of heart'; 'he studied to promote the welfare of mankind'. Others are offbeat and specific: he is congratulated for being on friendly terms with a better class of person, such as Wordsworth, Humphry Davy, Southey and Coleridge, and for bringing them to Nether Stowey.

One item is mystifying: his 'masculine intellect'. In the early nineteenth century surely that is just what a *man* would be expected to have; if it were otherwise the fact would probably not be mentioned on a plaque. The explanation, I think, comes two lines later: 'his originality and grasp of mind counterbalanced the deficiencies of early education'. We are, prematurely, in Samuel Smiles territory. Poole's father was a tanner who did not hold with book-learning. His son was a tanner too, but he did, and he put his belief heroically into practice, without apparently neglecting his trade.

Descriptions of him do suggest a self-educated man: the loud voice, the overbearing manner at the parish pump, and the tendency to call people damned fools. But he was a good man, in the sense that you mentioned him in your will if you wanted anything done; De Quincey said that nearly every man who died in Nether

Stowey appointed Poole guardian to his children.

He really did bring Coleridge to Nether Stowey. They met in 1794 when Poole was twenty-nine and Coleridge twenty-two, and discovered sympathies in common: for Pantisocracy, and for the French Revolution, of which both men, like Wordsworth, thought well until things went too far. Coleridge quickly became devoted to him and was overjoyed at the idea of living near him. When plans for the occupation of the cottage were held up he imagined Poole was showing reluctance and became hysterical.

Once settled in the cottage Coleridge wrote an extraordinary series of letters to Poole. The extraordinary thing about them was not the content, which was autobiographical and important though not always true, but the fact that they were written at all when the person addressed was living just over the garden wall.

The cottage in which Coleridge lived for three happy (for him) years must have been rather pretty, with a thatched roof, seemly proportions, a stream running in front of it and a flight of steps up to the door. Today nobody would give it a second glance if it was not for the Coleridge connection. The roof is no longer thatched and has been raised, giving the little house a surprised look, which could be whimsically accounted for by its directly facing The Ancient Mariner, an old pub which has been tricked out with a false front that does not suit it. A more agreeable view would have been the Congregational Church which for over a century was part of the outlook, but it has come and gone since Coleridge's time, which makes life seem very transitory.

In a poem written at Nether Stowey and addressed to Rev. George Coleridge, his brother, Coleridge refers depressingly to the cottage as a 'lowly shed', but this was, I think, part of the lowlier-than-thou attitude which he frequently adopted when speaking to his Ottery St Mary relatives. Towards them and his birthplace his feelings were so mixed that it would be simplistic to call them ambiguous.

To find any expression of contentment in the poetry of these three years one has to grope through the romantic self-pity, the childishness, the fear, the phoney homesickness, and especially the conviction that all laws applicable equally to all men – from Sod's and Murphy's to Archimedes' Principle and the Second Law of Thermodynamics – vented their fiercest equality on the hapless head of Samuel Taylor Coleridge. That done, one arrives at bright glimpses of happiness.

The Quantocks

'Well, they are gone and here I must remain', the first line of 'The Lime-Tree Bower my Prison', is the voice of the child, cross because the others have left him in the garden with his scalded foot, to 'wander in gladness' over the Quantocks. Yet before the poem has ended the acknowledgement of present beauty breaks right through the peevishness, as the beauty of the water-snakes was to break through the more desperately evil mood of the Ancient Mariner.

> Nor in this bower,
> This little lime-tree bower, have I not marked
> Much that has soothed me. Pale beneath the blaze
> Hung the transparent foliage; and I watched
> Some broad and sunny leaf, and love to see
> The shadow of the leaf and stem above
> Dappling its sunshine. And that walnut tree
> Was richly tinged, and a deep radiance lay
> Full on the ancient ivy, which usurps
> Those fronting elms, and now the blackest mass
> Makes their dark branches gleam a lighter hue
> Through the late twilight: and though now the bat
> Wheels silent by, and not a swallow twitters,
> Yet still the solitary humble-bee
> Sings in the bean-flower.

'Fears in Solitude' is even more explicit; the meditative joy he experienced in his own cottage garden becomes almost apocalyptic rapture as he looks down on his home from the Quantocks. He has been walking there to contemplate a fear which, though glistening and flaring with romanticism, sprang from a real enough danger: that of a French invasion.

> And now, beloved Stowey! I behold
> Thy church-tower and, methinks, the four huge elms
> Clustering, which mark the mansion of my friend;
> And close behind them, hidden from my view,
> Is my own lowly cottage, where my babe
> And my babe's mother dwell in peace. With light
> And quickened footsteps thitherward I tend.

This is all very different from his earlier descriptions of his first home in Ottery St Mary. Except that Poole's house was no more a mansion than Coleridge's was a shed, the view is accurately portrayed. There probably really were four elms in Poole's garden, no more no less. In his poems about his birthplace, for which he professed fervent enthusiasm, he trebled the size of the Otter and saw vast plains where none were or ever had been.

Before Coleridge had been in his cottage a year William and Dorothy Wordsworth came into the Quantocks. They came from Dorset, having decided they wanted to be nearer Coleridge, whom Wordsworth had first met in 1795; and Poole found them a house too: Alfoxden (Alfoxton) Park near Holford a little way up the Quantocks. It was quite a large house (Dove Cottage must later have seemed painfully cramped), early eighteenth-century and handsome, its entrance looking up to the hills and the other side out to the Bristol Channel.

What happened to Coleridge in the next two years is so important that his cottage at Nether Stowey, whatever it looks like, should be an object of pilgrimage as long as shrines and pilgrims exist and make sense. He was probably no more influenced by Wordsworth than Wordsworth was by him, although he admitted to feeling 'a little man by his side'. Neither could their close friendship exactly be called collaboration, for nothing commonly inspired or even equally balanced came out of it; *Lyrical Ballads* was not only the work of two completely different men, but of one far more than the other. Yet during the days of their walking and talking together in the Quantocks, Coleridge wrote infinitely better poetry than he had done before. Or ever would again; perhaps he came into his full knowledge of the Vast, as he called it, too soon.

Both poets had unusually carrying voices, as we know and as they discovered to their cost from the rumour that got around of their being spies. Poor Wordsworth was already being accused of living with '*a Woman who passes for his Sister*'. Incestuous, in fact, he may well have been, but almost certainly not an enemy agent. So many malicious and sharp-eared reports came steadily in from the good people of the Quantocks – Christopher Trickie (piously alleged to be the original of Simon Lee, which would be ironical if true), a halfwit called Mogg and others – that a detective was sent down from London to investigate the 'Rascalls', who by this time were said to include Thomas Poole, on account of his protection of 'Mr Coldridge'. The detective, though discovering the suspects to be 'a Sett of violent Democrats', sensibly concluded that there was nothing in the espionage theory, especially after he had heard Trickie's story that some French people had been asking if the brook outside his house (a very modest stream) was navigable to the sea.

The Wordsworths had first started the suspicions, a contemporary letter reveals, by going out at night carrying camp stools, and a portfolio for entering observations 'which they had been heard to say were almost finished' and that 'they should be rewarded for them'. But according to Coleridge, explaining the affair years later in *Biographia Literaria*, the key piece of evidence had been that in the course of his lusty conversations with Wordsworth about philosophy he had frequently been heard to speak of one Spy Nozy.

For nearly two centuries Coleridge's voice has been quite a legend among both those who knew him and those who had no such opportunity. Hazlitt declared that 'his voice rolled on the ear like a pealing organ and its sound alone was the music of thought'. Virginia Woolf made sensitive play with the notion that his 'spoken words still reverberate so that as we enter his radius he seems not a man, but a swarm, a cloud, a buzz of words, darting this way and that, clustering, quivering and hanging suspended'. Keats, who met him out walking near Highgate one Sunday, though he uses no explicit simile makes him sound like a brass band on the march: 'I heard his voice as he came towards me. I heard it as he moved away. I had heard it all the interval, if it may be called so.'

What Keats heard the Quantock villagers must have heard; and one does not have to be as sensitive as Virginia Woolf still to hear something of the sound as one walks in the streets of Nether Stowey and particularly among the hills. It is easy to work out the path that Coleridge and the Wordsworths must have followed to visit each other, and to guess their walks, whether taken for pure pleasure, or to fetch the eggs and bread from Holford Combe or to sign an appeal at Crowcombe.

They had chosen their environment well, all of them. The Quantocks are the most shapely hills I know. The valleys and hollows are wooded and the lower slopes have been ploughed and planted since the days of the earliest settlers, but the higher slopes have never been cultivated and for the most part are still gracefully bare. We can see the routes that those eighteenth-century walkers must have taken across the sheep-tracks, the grazing land and the ancient army-paths of the ridgeway.

In the *Alfoxden Journal* Dorothy Wordsworth gives us all the description we need of the Quantocks. It is not a systematic account. The wild eyes on which everybody commented – pleasantly or unpleasantly – glanced and that was enough.

The Quantocks

Walked upon the hill-tops; followed the sheep tracks till we overlooked the larger combe. Sat in the sunshine. The distant sheep-bells; the sound of the stream; the woodman winding along the half-marked road with his laden pony; locks of wool still spangled with the dewdrops; the blue-grey sea, shaded with immense masses of cloud, not streaked; the sheep glittering in the sunshine. Returned through the wood.

She is not always specific about place names, but when today one is walking through Shervage Wood, Holford Fields, Willoughby Cleeve or on Longstone Hill the terrain is vividly recognizable. I was in Shervage Wood recently and thought I had never seen so much holly in my life, and all so straggling and unsculptured. When I got home I consulted the *Journal* which I had not read properly since student days. Dorothy Wordsworth is fascinated by holly; she sees its boughs thickened with snow, its berries bright on the winter earth, its leaves patched with light in summer, its immobility in a high wind and convulsions in heavy rain, its benevolent power to shelter humans and donkeys.

Poole is often present in the *Alfoxden Journal*: 'Found Tom Poole in the parlour. He drank tea with us.' Coleridge is always there, even when in fact he was not. Three times Dorothy wrote 'walked with Coleridge' during a week when he is known to have been in Bristol. The obvious explanation is that she had mistaken the date, or that, in the relevant letters from Bristol, he had; he could never remember his own birthday. But I like to think there is a more interesting explanation. As Coleridge walked he talked, and when he talked a response was not always necessary, not often possible; so how natural that Dorothy Wordsworth, hearing with affection and respect the echo of a voice which can still be heard in those parts, should believe him to be beside her.

She was not overpowered by his company. In spite of her devotion to the men to whom she believed she should, in love or friendship, devote herself, she probably realised that the observations she made in her journals, and perhaps spoke aloud at the time, were usually much better worded than their versions, as they eventually appeared in poems. On March 7, 1798 she wrote:

One only leaf upon the top of a tree – the sole remaining leaf – danced round and round like a rag blown by the wind.

This sight appeared in Coleridge's 'Christabel' but gravely weakened by romanticism, verbosity and an uninteresting rhythm.

166

The one red leaf, the last of its clan,
That dances as often as dance it can,
Hanging so light, and hanging so high
On the topmost twig that looks up at the sky.

At the turn of the century the story of Coleridge and the Wordsworths moved away from Somerset; they had more than half their
lives still to live. *Lyrical Ballads* remains as a public monument to
the Nether Stowey years but not, sadly, as a precious private
memory to the writers. In *Biographia Literaria* Coleridge, though still
affirming Wordsworth's greatness, declares that he never con-
curred with Wordsworth's ideas about the *Ballads*, especially as set
out in the preface to the second edition, but in fact objected to them
on grounds which he goes on very firmly to state. Had these words
been read and understood by the *opera buffa* eavesdroppers who
had lurked behind bushes in the Quantocks at the time of the Spy
Nosy affair, they would have been met with incredulity.

Thomas Poole remained in Nether Stowey, keeping the fitful but
genuine regard of his protégés, but except for the tablet in the
church there is no memorial to him. He moved from the house
with the four elms where he was living when Coleridge was in the
cottage. It now has a ladies' hairdresser in part of it but no plaque.

If it comes to that there are not many signs of Coleridge himself. Yet he is still remembered in the land. At Clevedon Court,
now in Avon, then in Somerset, there is a showy painting by
Edward Villiers Rippingille, first exhibited in 1824. It is called 'The
Travellers' Breakfast' and has aimed at including as many great
men and members of the Elton family as could plausibly be depicted
in one room at the same time. Coleridge is there, of course; he had
connections with Clevedon Court: the Reverend Sir Abraham Elton
had lent him a cottage in Clevedon for his honeymoon. He is
holding out a boiled egg which was either high or not cooked to
his liking. Wordsworth is flaring his nostrils over it but appears not
to be paying much attention. A woman said to be Dorothy wears
an expression suggesting that if she could be bothered to move her
hands she would wash them of the whole affair. Southey is ogling
a girl; Humphry Davy is warming a fat thigh at the fire. So the four
famous men mentioned with such approbation in Thomas Poole's
memorial in Nether Stowey are all present. Not all the figures have
been identified, but I have never heard it suggested that one of
them was Thomas Poole.

Blackdown Hills and Wellington Monument

Chapter 12

AGAINST THE SKY

Bury the Great Duke
  With an empire's lamentation,
Let us bury the Great Duke
  To the noise of the mourning of a mighty nation,
Mourning when their leaders fall,
Warriors carry the warrior's pall,
And sorrow darkens hamlet and hall.

TENNYSON'S 'Ode on the Death of the Duke of Wellington' – written in 1852 and one of his first as Poet Laureate – is wonderfully bad as a poem. Most of it comes out of the same drawer as the works of the great-souled William McGonagall. It bears, in fact, a striking resemblance to the Scottish poet's 'The Funeral of the German Emperor' written some three decades later. (I have no idea, without looking it up, *which* German Emperor, and I think dear McGonagall may not have been too worried either.) The two gain from being read together.

A man's achievements, however, can be celebrated in other ways, and the Wellington monument is wonderfully good. After the usual wrangling, back-biting and cheese-paring, it took the form of an obelisk made of ashlar, designed by Thomas Lee of Barnstaple, an architect who had once worked with Sir John Soane and who also built Arlington Court in Devon, and set up against the sky on the Blackdown Hills in Somerset to become part of one of the most beautiful places in the world.

This happened in 1817, two years after Waterloo. The fact that the Duke was honoured in this way thirty-five years before his death has resulted in an interesting dissimilarity between his monument and that of Admiral Hardy on the Dorset coast. Hardy's finest hour, as the public would see it, was Trafalgar, ten years before the Duke's, yet because his monument was not put up till 1844 appearances would suggest that he flourished a great while after Wellington. Whole ages of architectural change seem to separate them rather than one generation. Wellington got one of the best styles, Hardy one of the worst. Wellington's memorial is elegant and imposing; Hardy's is lumpy and truculent. It is tempting, if fanciful and class-conscious, to see a certain suitability about the difference: Wellington was an aristocrat, Hardy a yeoman. Yet the difference is mainly disconcerting, for the two men were similar in the qualities for which they were being celebrated and to an extent in appearance: they were strong-featured, bold and clever. In one point, however, the monuments are alike: the statue of the hero that was to top the whole thing off is in both cases missing to this day.

Whereas in his Ode Tennyson, in spite of all the references to Waterloo, was naturally thinking of the Great Duke as 'the good grey head which all men knew', Thomas Lee was inspired by a head which was less grey and less soberly good; though as to that even in 1852 Tennyson seems to have been afraid that cats might yet come out of the bag and put him in a weak position: 'Whatever record leap to light/He never shall be shamed.' Lee's obelisk is slim and flexible, which indeed it needs to be, given the winds of the Blackdown Hills.

To call the history of the monument chequered would be not only a cliché but an inadequate one, for most of the circumstances of its making were farcically chaotic. There was mild inanity from the start in the Duke's name. No peer can have selected a title for less solid reasons. The Viscount, Earl, Marquess and Duke of Wellington which Arthur Wellesley successively became – and rapidly too; he was already Duke at the time of Waterloo – picked the place name because the first syllable was the same as his family name and because his ancestors were flimsily associated with the hamlet of Wellesley in the parish of Wells, Somerset. His European titles were more purposefully chosen but unfortunately carried a suggestion of comic opera: Duke of Ciudad Rodrigo, Duke of Vittoria, Marquess of Torres Vedras, Count Vimeiro, Prince of Waterloo.

His relationship with his English town did nothing to justify the choice. He was given property in the neighbourhood to create a show of suitability but in fact he visited it only once. The love which towed his carriage through the cheering streets in 1819 turned to hate in 1832 at the time of the Reform Bill. The people burned his effigy and let off aggressive fireworks. Somebody painted in a devil on the sign of the inn that bore his name and added some simple but offensive dialogue. 'Will you vote for the Bill now?' demands the devil preparing to drag him off. 'Yes, I will,' says Wellington.

In 1817 the foundation stone was laid. It must have been a fine sight with all the civic and military dignitaries; and a fine sound too with the Clayhidon band leading the mile-long procession and a crowd of ten thousand singing 'God Save the King' at the top of the hill and marching down again to get drunk.

But financially the response began to tail off. Such economies as reducing the proposed four sides of the column to three did not meet the case. Continuous appeals for funds tantalizingly brought in rather less than was needed. The momentum was lost, and after ten wearisome years everybody walked away from the column, leaving it unfinished up in the rain and wind and fog of the Blackdown Hills. Seventeen years later still it was struck by lightning and badly damaged.

What the Duke himself thought of this prolonged tragi-comedy I do not know. It might have brought sheltered vulnerable spirits to the verge of breakdown, but no doubt Wellington of Waterloo was made of sterner stuff. In any case, like the lovely woman who stooped to folly, found too late that men betray, and realised that the only way to make something positive out of it was to die, in 1852 the Duke brought the situation to a head. A genuine piety was rekindled, fanned by his consistent benevolence to the town of Wellington in subscribing to new schools and so on. More fund-raising appeals were launched. Work on the monument was resumed. It was brought up to the handsome height of 170 feet and given a pointed top. This is much as we see it today except that inevitable restoration works, particularly those of 1890, have added a few feet to its height.

All this may sound more melancholy than farcical and seem to postulate some Great Nanny in the sky who tells her charges that nobody is going to look at *them*. But the story of the guns is indisputably comic. Twenty-four brass cannon, said to have been taken at Waterloo, were to be sent by sea from Woolwich Arsenal to be installed round the column. In the event fifteen *iron* guns were unloaded at Exeter in 1818. They had never been anywhere near Waterloo but were part of a consignment ordered by Catherine the Great and made in Scotland before the end of the eighteenth century. At Exeter they stayed, for nearly a hundred years, the Monument Committee refusing to pay for their transport and Exeter Corporation threatening to sell them. They became quite a *cause célèbre*, and their plight, about which it was all too easy to become sentimental, invested them with a personality. At the time of the 1890 restorations Edward Jeboult, a citizen of Taunton, made up a song for them: 'The Lament of the Monument Guns'.

When we were made a present of
Twas named as a condition
That we should hereafter occupy
An honourable position . . .

Our fellow guns have elsewhere met
With flattering receptions,
But here we lie the victims of
The cruellest deceptions.

Exeter was unmoved. It was not until 1910 that they sent on four of the guns, which were arranged round the monument and, according to a contemporary sketch, looked very nice. They are not there now. In the Second World War they were commandeered for scrap metal, like the railings and gates of all the rest of us, but were never used. They lie buried at Watchet.

The Wellington Monument can be seen from most of Somerset. It can also be seen from the Black Mountains of Wales and from the Haldon Hills on the far side of the Exe, well into Devon. My own favourite view is from the back, if a three-sided obelisk can be said to have a back that is, from the ridge road that crosses Luppitt Common, a few miles out of Honiton, and runs straight towards the Blackdown Hills on their less steep side. The length of the hills forms the horizon and it is easy to see them as the right and proper boundary between Somerset and Devon, which they were before the recent manipulation. The road over the Common looks over the valley of the Culm with Hemyock to the west, this side of the river, and Clayhidon to the east, beyond it; across all the farms and the fields rising up to the far ridge, and there against the sky is the Wellington Monument looking away into Somerset.

When I was young I once climbed the 235 steps to the top; but never again. The view from the base is magnificent enough

Cheddar Gorge

nowadays. The Vale of Taunton Deane lies immediately below at the foot of a steep heavily-wooded scarp and the two branches of the wetlands divide into their valleys, one running westwards south of the Brendons and the Quantocks and the other north of the Quantocks to the coast.

Into the scene from the west comes the M5, along the track of the much earlier road that brought Devonians out to seek their fortunes. It sparkles and hums through the trees, by-passing Wellington, passing the church of West Buckland on its isolated little knoll, by-passing Taunton and disappearing again on its way to industry, commerce and worldly pleasure.

To the north-east lie the Mendips and Cheddar Gorge, all inky and two-dimensional at that distance, with the Poldens in front, a smaller range that must have risen bravely out of the sea and the marshes and been a refuge to many travellers and fighters. But the glory of the view is the great cumulus of the western hills: the Brendons, the Quantocks and Exmoor. They are close enough to have texture: the grazing commons on top of the Quantocks look rough and scratchy. They are close enough not to merge into each other but to appear in their personal shapes and characters: Dunkery Hill though high enough to overtop the Brendons is seen as stocky and wide rather than towering.

If the chief reason for putting a building up against the sky is to honour a man, the second is that a man wishes to give himself something to look at. This is not an irreligious criticism of God's creative powers, almost the contrary: God has made his eyes; he will make some worthy view. Others may call it a folly; he tends to think of it as an eye-opener.

There had been Bonds in Purbeck as long as there had been Starkadders at Cold Comfort Farm, that is always. They made bricks, they bred sheep, they cast bells. But it was not till the end of the seventeenth century that they became the Bonds of Creech Grange. The house was built at least a hundred and fifty years earlier. Though countless improvements have left it looking rather bad-tempered, it has more distinction and unity than its history of patching and faking would suggest. The nineteenth-century Elizabethan east front is made of Portland stone ashlar which was no more available at the time of its real building than the potato in its kitchens nor the smell of tobacco in its gardens, yet it is beautiful, in its wooded valley.

In 1740 Denis Bond, healthily conscious of the Zeitgeist which was throwing up eye-catchers all over Europe, built the first one in Dorset. He may have been following the advice of the psalmist too, for he certainly had to lift up his eyes unto the hills to see it, about 650 feet in fact. The ridge on which Grange Arch, also known as Bond's Folly, stands is part of the Purbeck Hills and the slope swings up right in front of the house so he must have had to tilt back his head as well. He chose precisely the best spot. From the road which cuts across the estate about thirty yards away from the south front of the house, the view of the arch is not quite right, but from the drawing room windows it must be perfect.

The grounds starts to rise at this lower part of the road. A stretch of tall grass, full of buttercups in June, leads up between two rather aimless urns to a row of trees which at this season, except for the occasional flash of a car, hide the road that now zig-zags back across the property again. Beyond, the trees crowd over the hillside, some conifers but mostly deciduous: oaks, chestnuts and beeches.

I do not know if owners of eye-catchers ever want to stand beside them and look back or down at their houses. If Denis Bond never did this he was missing a treat. For today's tourist a rough track, to the west of the picnic area and the red flags threatening gunnery practice, first shows the arch from the side, gleaming palely and standing like a ghost at attention. Seen at its full width, it is a handsome totally useless structure with three openings, Venetian in design with crenellation and four pretty little pyramids, excluding nothing, admitting nothing, and joined to nothing at either end. It is purely something for Mr Bond to look at, and naturally its more ornate side is turned towards him.

It is placed accurately on the side of the ridge nearer the house. The ridge itself is as thin and round as a rolling pin in the middle of more solid formations. The Purbeck Hills, a chalk downland with the occasional crop of clover, are very green compared with the black fragments of heath, the last of Egdon, to the north. To the south are cultivated fields tilting inland on the top of the cliffs and then the sea itself, with Lulworth Cove to the west and St Aldhelm's Head to the east. As we stood there two cormorants took a short cut across Purbeck, from Warbarrow to Studland Bay and their stronghold at Old Harry Rocks.

The third reason for placing a building against the sky is that it may serve some practical purpose: as a lookout or a landmark or a means of communication. What purpose Bruton Dovecote was originally meant to serve is debatable. It was not intended to be a

Pepperbox Hill, near Salisbury

Grange Arch, Creech

dovecote. There are considerably fewer than a hundred nests in it which would not have housed a viable number of birds, if they were to be used for food. The point would of course be irrelevant if it were not for the received opinion that the dovecote once belonged to the abbey established on the south side of Bruton in the early days of the Norman Conquest. Doves kept for ornament do not sound any more monkish than would the presence of inedible goldfish in the abbey pond. In any case the tower would have been unnecessarily far from the kitchen.

Authorities seem to agree that the tower was built in the sixteenth century. If so, and if by the monks, it must have been one of the abbey's last improvements for it was duly dissolved by Henry VIII. The king sold it to the Berkeleys who turned it to splendid secular use. They did everything handsomely and may very well have installed some doves simply because they looked pretty.

The abbey was pulled down two centuries ago. The Berkeley who owned it at the end of the eighteenth century died without an heir and it passed to the Berkeley Castle branch of the family. They did not want it and so sold it to the Hoares of Stourhead. After a decade they decided they did not want it either and demolished it.

The tower remains. It stands on top of a high pasture above the town, isolated from its present life though it must have been better integrated in the days when Bruton was an important though small market town which acted as distribution centre to the region. The view from the tower is quite unlike that from the monument in the western hills and the folly near the Dorset coast. Bruton is near the Wiltshire border but the dovecote seems to look west into Somerset along the southern arc, the narrow forty-five-mile stretch of rich farmland which reaches as far as the Vale of Taunton Deane and ends not far from the Devon border, more or less below the Wellington monument in fact.

The tower is partly ruined; its four gables are no longer connected by a roof. It is often dramatic against a stormy sky, for the rainfall is heavy around Bruton, and its hilltop though relatively unimposing can be as windy as the Blackdowns. Inside the building, the mystery about what it once was is complicated by traces of habitation: remains of a fireplace and a first floor. But mystery alone cannot account for the smell of fear. It is quite illogical, in view of previous arguments, to think of doves being caught and killed, but I could not help imagining someone with a net coming in, shutting the door and blocking all the escape routes, and sweeping the net about in the

Bruton Dovecote

dark while hundreds of terrified birds blundered about in what they had thought of as their home.

Two motives have been suggested for the building of the Pepperbox which stands on Brickworth Down, five miles south-west of Salisbury, and they are not mutually exclusive. One is that it was to be a vantage point from which women could watch men hunting animals. This might well be so. It is an elegant little red-brick tower, gracefully patterned, octagonal in shape with a pyramid roof. The top windows, most of them blocked up now, would have given a prospect of some of the most famous chases in southern England: to the west lies Cranborne, to the south the New Forest. It would have been a distant prospect, it is true, but on a still day the watchers might have heard the baying and the yelling.

Even if nothing came into sight, on a reasonably clear day they could have amused themselves by watching the shipping in the Solent, or simply have enjoyed the sight of what was moving in the wind on the beautiful chalk ridge around them: wild grasses, dogwood, juniper, cowslips and purple orchids.

The alternative name of the Pepperbox is Eyre's Folly, which leads to the other possible motive. The tower was built in 1606, and the Eyre of that day was Gyles, whose memorial tablet, in the church of Whiteparish at the foot of the downs, shows him to have been a local landowner of tempestuous character. The inscription mentions his 'laudable opposition' to every monarch in whose reign he lived. He sounds like a mirror image of the Vicar of Bray.

It is not too surprising to find a lively legend which says he erected the tower with the sole purpose of spiting his neighbour, Sir Thomas Gorges, who built Longford Castle in 1591. Sir Thomas seems to have been an equally unbridled character: a man of notions, swept into action by the occult and by anything curious. He designed his castle according to some mystical plan, in a triangular shape which in those days was so eccentric as to be almost scandalous.

The plump towers of Longford Castle today look romantically handsome and harmless in their wooded valley between Brickworth Down and Salisbury, with the cathedral spire and the Plain rising up behind them. But they may well have annoyed Gyles Eyre; almost everything seemed to. And it is quite believable that he should have planned a tower 156 feet above sea level to aggravate his neighbour, both by being able to look down on him and by providing him with an eye-catcher which he did not want but could see out of almost every window.

Above Eype Mouth, Golden Cap Estate

Chapter 13

LAND OF OPEN GLORY

I TAKE no credit for the title of this chapter. It is lifted from an article in the *Radio Times* of mid-August 1984, the purpose of which was to introduce a broadcast with a less skittish title, *The Countryside in Trust*, which spoke about the open spaces administered by the National Trust. The property chiefly discussed was the Golden Cap Estate, which starts at Charmouth on the Dorset coast and continues east for about five miles to Eype Mouth, south-west of Bridport. The Estate consists of 1,974 acres of coastland, the gradual acquisition of which was part of Enterprise Neptune.

The coast of Dorset is a disconcerting piece of land. It can collapse under you physically. Responsible guide books carry vivid warnings about crumbling and sliding cliffs, and solid advice about what to do if the worst happens. Soon after the stalwart red cliffs of Devon have turned white, at Beer, and from the point where the Dorset Coast Path leaves Lyme Regis, we are told to prepare to meet our God, if not by our guide books, by the signs of doom in the terrain itself: fissures and cracks, a detour around Timber Hill, and, when the diversion works back to the cliff, a downward and backward view of the missing path that caused the detour, disintegrating helplessly but obstinately in the sea.

The Coast Path enters the Golden Cap Estate below Stonebarrow Hill, and here the walker is further scared by the sight of Cain's Folly. I do not know the true derivation of the name but the suggestions are right, for as Cain was a killer so must this landslide have been, or perhaps a Samson dragging others down in its fall. More benevolent in appearance are the low cliffs of the immediate approach to Seatown from the west. They have slipped just as ostentatiously but not as far and have come to rest not in the sea,

Stonebarrow Down, Golden Cap

where they would hardly be at rest long, but on the beach, just behind the holidaymakers. The blue lias spreads gracefully on the beige and grey pebbles, looking no more violent than an overlong skirt. It is a most beautiful colour, blue not bluish, but so delicate that it makes the scene look hazy even on a clear day.

The Dorset coast is startling in other ways. It has been said of the English sealine as a whole that a geologist confronted with a painting of coastal scenery could place the subject within a mile or two. In Dorset it could be within a yard or two, I imagine. The rocks have tumbled about in a way which results not so much in chaos as in anarchy. Each piece, each unit, has a distinct and disruptive identity of its own.

Chesil Bank – ceosil is the Anglo-Saxon word for gravel – just beyond the Golden Cap Estate to the east has through the ages cast its strange personality over the whole area. Among other things it was a weapon. In the early years of the first century AD, the Durotriges, a British tribe who occupied most of the Iron Age hill-forts in the region, were perpetually poised to beat off the Dumnonii, the men of Devon just across the western border. In the end the Durotriges, looking the wrong way, were overtaken by a worse enemy: the Second Legion under the command of the future emperor Vespasian. The story goes that with the Dumnonii in mind the Durotriges had prepared themselves with thousands of flint pebbles, to be used as sling shots, that they had collected from Chesil Bank. In the event they had time to use only a few of them. They died beside piles of their native stones.

However little one knows about the art of slinging one can be sure that the pebbles were small, for they must have been gathered from the west end of the Bank. This long ridge of shingle – a rampart in places – stretches offshore from the Isle of Portland to a point nearly twenty miles to the west, well beyond Abbotsbury where it joins the regular coastline. Between it and the mainland lies a tidal lagoon called the Fleet. This is extraordinary but not exceptional. What does seem to be unique is that the pebbles are systematically graded in size: from large as tennis balls in the east to small as marbles in the west. (To walk the whole length of the Bank starting at Portland would be like approaching a roundabout which attempts to slow the motorist down by means of those yellow lines with diminishing spaces between them.) There appears to be no explanation, and indeed there is further mystification in the rumour that the pebbles *under* the water *increase* in size from east to west.

Eype Mouth

Golden Cap

Chesil Bank is not only a weapon but a protector and a destroyer. Without its shelter the tall golden sandstone cliffs beyond West Bay would have gone the way of Cain's Folly long ago. And without its presence many fine ships would have sailed on. The Dorset coast all the way along has as dreadful a reputation as the north coast of Cornwall in the nineteenth century when the succession of wrecks broke the wits of Parson Hawker of Morwenstow into a frenzy of anger and compassion. But Chesil Bank is the most vicious part of it.

It has often been blamed for the loss, with all hands, of the *Earl of Abergavenny*, an East Indiaman bound for Bengal in 1805 under the command of Captain John Wordsworth, the poet's brother, but though no doubt wreckage and corpses were washed up on to Chesil it was in fact another bank further offshore that the ship struck. But it has taken a frightening toll all the same. In the course of the great gales that have been blowing from the south-west across Lyme Bay for ever, Chesil Bank has been regularly picking off ships of every kind, but it was the uppercase Great Gales of 1824 and 1838 that turned it into a mass murderer.

In 1838 it accounted for the *Arethusa*, the schooners *Columbine* and *Mary Ann*, the Weymouth sloop *Dove*, the French smack *Le Jean Bart* and the Swedish barque *Louise*. The Great Gale of 1824 was equally destructive, but there was one bizarre incident that possibly had a happy ending. The wave that seized the government sloop *Ebenezer* hurled it so high up the Bank that it came down on the other side, and, with a little hauling from the helpful natives who always turned up in droves on such occasions, it arrived in the safe waters of the lagoon; with its crew still aboard, one hopes, and of course the government officials too.

Those who are not aroused by the statistics of shipwreck could read *Moonfleet* by J. Meade Falkner, a late Victorian novel of adventure which has some breathtaking descriptions of peril not only on the sea but specifically on Chesil Bank, lightly disguised in the book as Moonfleet Beach.

Surprisingly for 1898, the goodies are men more often presented as baddies: smugglers, and proud of it. 'All my life I have served the Contraband,' says the older of the two heroes, as though he were speaking of the Muzzy Guides. To cut a long story short, two of the Boys in the Contraband, after many tribulations abroad, are being deported to Java as convicts when their brig is wrecked on Moonfleet Beach. As they are driven towards the shore the narrator describes what we the readers recognize as the characteristic white arc of Chesil in a storm.

> In the mist to which we were making a sternboard I saw a white line like a fringe or valance to the sea; and then I looked to starboard, and there was the same white fringe, and then to larboard, and the white fringe was there too.

And he hears the voice of Chesil:

> the awful roar of the under-tow sucking back the pebbles on the beach . . . I wondered if any sat before their inland hearths this night, and hearing that far distant roar, would throw another log on the fire, and thank God they were not fighting for their lives in Moonfleet Bay.

The narrator, as I need hardly say, was rescued, by his friend, and prospered.

> And more than once I have stood rope in hand in that same awful place, and tried to save a struggling wretch; but never saw one come through the surf alive in such a night as he saved me.

The same sensible guide books that warn about the crumbling cliffs of Dorset give varying advice about searching for fossils among them. In the 1970s they pointed out to fossil-hunters that when dislodging rocks they should remember there might be people underneath. In any case they should not hammer away indiscriminately. One is reminded of Dickens's geologist Professor Dingo in *Bleak House* 'in his last illness when, his mind wandering, he insisted on keeping his little hammer under the pillow, and chipping at the countenances of his attendants.' In the 1980s digging for fossils is discouraged both informally and legally. Just picking them up is another matter.

This is quite easy to do. There can be no dispute about the plentiful presence of fossils all along the Golden Cap Estate, as indeed along the whole Dorset coast. Geological hammers such as Professor Dingo's can be bought at beach kiosks. There are fossil shops at the resorts. In *Dorset Coast Path* (1979) Brian Jackman uses images of cookery to describe the abundance. 'Sometimes these fossil remains occur in such numbers that whole strata are stuffed with shells as thick as currants in a Christmas pudding. Witness

Fossils, Dancing Ledge, Winspit

the Green Ammonite beds under Golden Cap.' Farther to the east, just beyond Eype Mouth 'we find green-grey Fuller's Earth clay at Watton Cliff *peppered* with belemnites, ammonites, rare brachiopods and brittle-starfish'.

The belemnite and the ammonite are the most common and the easiest to recognize. The belemnite is shaped like a bullet or a cigar; it was the skeleton of a squid-like creature. The ammonite is more picturesque. It is coiled and fluted. Visually it bears the same resemblance to a snail as a planisphere does to the globe.

There were no inhibitions about digging for fossils in the days of Mary Anning, who was born in Lyme Regis in 1799. In her strolls along the beach with her dog she did not realise she was walking on the prehistoric floor of Dorset, but in 1811 she did notice certain bones sticking out of Black Venn, a cliff between Lyme and Charmouth, and acted on her observation. She found some men to help her excavate the mass of blue lias in which the bones were embedded and so revealed to a startled world a skeleton thirty feet long. It is now in the British Museum but it did not get there immediately. The geologists, taken on the hop, needed time and much discussion to decide what place the creature occupied in natural history, let alone what to call it. The name ichthyosaurus was at last agreed on. But there was more to come, for Mary Anning went on to find the first specimen of plesiosaurus and then that of pterodactylus, a big-mouthed, web-winged character that must be one of the meanest dreams homo sapiens ever had.

To compare Mary Anning with Bernadette Soubirous would be to offend the devotees of either the one or the other, but I think there are profound resemblances. In that neither was male or middle class, they were both at a disadvantage from the start. But though they were uneducated in the conventional meaning of the word they had learned to trust the evidence of their senses. Mary knew she had seen something important and so did Bernadette, and they were unswerving in their declarations of what they had witnessed. For the general promulgation of their visions they had to depend entirely on others, and neither was treated with great personal respect in the process; in science and religion women were still handmaids. They both brought prosperity to their home towns, though Lourdes did better than Lyme Regis. The possibilities were there in Lyme: a local guide book said of Mary that 'her death was in a pecuniary sense a great loss to the place, as her presence attracted a large number of distinguished visitors'. But the beatific

190

vision snowballed to an extent that the scientific discovery, personally, did not.

Bernadette has churches. Mary Anning has a stained glass window. It was put in her parish church fifteen years after her death, by the Geological Society. This tribute has a fine illogicality considering the blow she administered to orthodox religion. Was there a stained glass window to Charles Darwin in the nineteenth century? But, in spite of the difference of their fortunes, there is a link between the two girls who went out into the country one day with open minds and open eyes and saw and believed things which affected the whole world.

You can get a good impression of the Golden Cap Estate as a whole by walking along the top of Stonebarrow Hill and on to Chardown Hill; in as far as any impression of the estate can be got at any one time, for the mists rise up from the sea with a speed which would be really dangerous on Dartmoor. Even here, it is disconcerting enough to doze for a while on a clear day and wake up wrapped in mist. Like Bertie Wooster, full many a glorious morning have I seen flatter the mountain top with sovereign eye and then turn into quite a nasty afternoon. The top of the Golden Cap is often, in fact, completely invisible from Chardown Hill thought it is less than a mile away.

The grassy downland of Stonebarrow and Chardown is blowy; the hedge along the top is driven right back by the prevailing wind from the sea. But it gives pleasant walking, not only to humans: one usually encounters a migration of black-stockinged sheep with devilish eyes and Christian behaviour grazing their way along, only to meet them grazing their way back a few hours later. The slopes of Stonebarrow Hill are scratchy with brambles and bracken and coarse golden grass. Chardown Hill is rough with heather and gorse.

Sounds travel. A gate far below clicks loudly as a group of quiet walkers comes up from Stanton St Gabriel; a dignified name for a Tudor farmhouse, a cottage and the ruins of a thirteenth-century church: the remains of what was quite a prosperous village when the old coaching road from Exeter to Dorset passed through it. The thud of horses' hoofs is loud even when no horses have come into sight. They would test the skill of old Colonel Sapt in *The Prisoner of Zenda* who by putting his ear to the ground could tell how many horses and, by the manner of their riding, the probable identity of the horsemen. Or perhaps, as they nearly always turn out to be from some dude stable, it would be all too easy.

The coast path crosses the lower slopes of Golden Cap, but another very good approach to it is from Langdon Hill, to the north-east. A path goes round the hill through the 48-acre wood of beech, Corsican pine and Scots pine: a beautiful walk in itself with seats at the best viewpoints. It is a good opportunity to get a proper view of Chideock (one of the few genuine Celtic place-names in Dorset) on the A35, which as you go through it with the other traffic is impossible. From Langdon Hill even the A35 looks quite romantic as it swings up out of the village and away east through the gap between Quarry Hill and Frogmore.

At the end of the wood there is a short climb across grassland to the top of Golden Cap: strenuous but nothing like as drawn-out as what awaits the walkers on the coast path, soon seen toiling away below. Golden Cap, at 619 feet, is the highest cliff on the south coast of England. Sounds come up as they do on Stonebarrow. From a field a long way down, where some paramilitary organization involving small boys has encamped, there rises the sudden sound of a bugle as though Vespasian was alive again.

It might well be death to peer over the top of Golden Cap. The soles of one's feet are warily conscious of the coloured layers that lead up to the glowing crown, co-habiting but never integrating. But the more distant views are ravishing, and safe. To the immediate east, Seatown, it is true, is not very pleasing. Like Eype Mouth, further along, it is a point of access to the beach rather than an elegant resort. But, beyond Seatown, the coast path soars by way of Doghouse Hill to Thorncombe Beacon, only a hundred feet or so lower than Golden Cap. It is a noble outline.

In detail it is even richer in being the home of wildlife – badgers, foxes, hares – that can sometimes be seen at close quarters for they are unusually bold. It is one of the last resorts of what Christopher Wordsworth in a *Sunday Times Magazine* article charmingly referred to as 'that harmless ancient Briton, the slow-worm'. The Beacon, like the rest of the Estate, is full of birds, especially the kestrel – beak down like Concorde – and the buzzard, and that other bird whose reckless eyes and determined way with chaffinches and even blackbirds make sense of the Duke of Wellington's advice to Queen Victoria: 'Try sparrowhawks, ma'am.'

The view from Golden Cap gives the historical imagination much to work on. To look out across the Channel can be to see the terrifying crescent of the Armada moving ponderously east through the blinding summer rain, coming in so close that the watchers on

Eggardon Hill

the clifftops – and Golden Cap must have looked like the pinhead of medieval speculation with myriads of angels crowded on to it – were convinced at one point that it was going to attack Weymouth. To the north, not far beyond the bounds of the Estate, the shapes of Coney's Castle and Lambert's Castle can, with faith and good weather, be seen; and, a little further east and as a rule more clearly, Eggardon Hill. It is easy to conjure up the whole chain of these Iron Age forts – thirty of them right across the county – where tribe fought against tribe until the Romans brought peace of a kind that they did not want, at a price they had never thought of paying.

Imagination of a more social kind is called for when it comes to the view, downwards and west, of what is the heart of the Golden Cap Estate: the farms and farmland of the little valleys enclosed by Stonebarrow Hill on the west and north, by Langdon Hill and Golden Cap on the east, and by the sea to the south. They are the most beautiful sight, the small irregular fields, all elbows and knees, and the banked hedges which we are used to in these parts but which make visitors exclaim. But there is more to it than that, as the radio programme *The Countryside in Trust* made clear. The question is: can productive farming co-exist with good conservation?

Richard North, writing in the autumn 1984 issue of *National Trust*, thinks it can. He is well aware of the difficulty: 'How to reconcile the needs of the farmer with those of landscape, plants and animals is a far more pressing problem for the Trust than it is for most landowners.' Yet he feels that new ideas are stirring according to which 'lower inputs of expensive chemical fertilizers and pesticides are seen as profitable, because though the end is lower output, each unit of production, each bushel or pint of crop, has cost so much less to get'. He foresees 'a new age of farming in which much of the landscape we are now desperate to preserve or re-instate (which is, roughly, the farmscape which existed, with regional variation, all over this country until World War II) may become desirable not merely for visitors but for farmers too'.

Chapter 14

THE LAST WORD

RALPH WIGHTMAN, loyal son of Wessex, published *Portrait of Dorset* in 1965. Since his death in 1971 there have been radical changes in the facts he so affectionately and scrupulously recorded, such as the vexatious – to most people – revision of the county boundaries. His book has been revised twice on this account, most recently by Roland Gant. But the final paragraph of this new edition contains a more important piece of news than any tinkerings, however irritating, with boundaries.

> Ralph Wightman would have rejoiced with Dorset and the nation as a whole at the news that Henry Ralph Bankes of Kingston Lacy House who died on 19 August 1981, left the whole estate – some twenty-five miles of Dorset's finest scenery, including Corfe Castle and village – to the National Trust which accepted officially this greatest ever bequest on 15 April 1982.

Every existing book on Wessex now bears or will soon be bearing this triumphant last word.

It is indeed a bequest to be celebrated, and at length. The county magazine *Dorset* in its 100th issue has given a full and mouth-watering account. The estate is vast: 16,000 acres, 25 square miles. The estate is varied. I dislike lists because they dragoon the imagination, but it would be a sickly imagination that would not stand up to a list like the following.

The Bankes Estate includes: a seventeenth-century mansion (Kingston Lacy) and a manor house dating from 1300 (Godlingston Manor); one of the most popular ruined castles in Europe (Corfe); a major Iron Age hill fort (Badbury Rings); prehistoric barrows (Nine Barrow Down and Straw Barrow); heathland and common

Kingston Lacy being restored

land, from wild to tame (Corfe Common, Cowgrove Common, Studland Heath, Holt Heath, Hartland Moor, God's Blessing Green); a sea coast, from inside Poole Harbour westward to well beyond Old Harry Rocks, with other areas at Dancing Ledge and Seacombe Cliff); geological features (the 400 tons of sandstone called Agglestone which somehow arrived in the middle of Studland Heath); cliff workings (Hedbury Quarry); and assorted curiosities, from a nudist beach to a London gas-lamp set on a prehistoric barrow to commemorate the piping of water to Swanage in 1892 (Ballard Down obelisk).

Kingston Lacy House was built in the 1660s for Sir Ralph Bankes. The architect he chose was Sir Roger Pratt, the first architect to be knighted. Kingston Lacy is his most important existing building and a perfect example of the Restoration house, in spite of its nineteenth-century modernization by Sir Charles Barry who covered the original redbrick with grey stone and altered a great deal else.

At present the house is closed to the public and until quite recently has been lost to sight behind scaffolding and tarpaulins. The contents went into store, so that the dry rot and the death watch beetle could be dealt with, and the discrepancy between the original brickwork and Barry's stone facing could be adjusted. The house will probably be fully open to the public in 1986, when we shall be able to see once more, under different management, the majestic staircase (Barry) with its Italianate wall-friezes and painted ceiling, and its half-landing with Marochetti's three life-size statues in bronze of Charles I, Sir John Bankes and Lady Bankes; the Library with the Guido Reni painting set into the ceiling; the Spanish Room with its disputed ceiling painting (Sansovino? Veronese?); the Saloon, its panels carved with fruit in the style of Grinling Gibbons and its ornate ceiling created by Barry, for here he did assert himself though he had less to do with the other main rooms.

Since the early pre-National Trust catalogue (price 2/–) some changes have been made with regard to the attributions of these paintings. *The Judgement of Solomon*, for example, once confidently declared to be the work of Giorgione, is nowadays considered to be by Sebastiano del Piombo. On the other hand, Titian's *Portrait of Francesco Savorgnan della Torre* has this year been re-authenticated for its appearance in the exhibition *The Genius of Venice* at the Royal Academy; that is to say, it may not be Francesco Savorgnan della Torre but it *is* Titian.

Kingston Lacy

There could be some surprises yet to come about the other paintings, but the names are most impressive: Rubens, Breughel, Rembrandt, Velasquez. The family portraits by Lely, Van Dyck, Romney, Zoffany and Lawrence, many of which were done in the house and are well documented, are almost certainly what they claim to be.

The art collection was to a great extent assembled by the nineteenth-century William John Bankes, often referred to journalistically as the greatest Bankes of them all. This is going rather far, though he certainly seems to have been an interesting man, if only in the wholeheartedness with which in youth and prime he wore the Romantic uniform. He appears to have been as eager as his friend Byron to be considered mad, bad and dangerous to know, and to have put a great deal of effort into making himself too hot to handle.

His indirect descendant Viola Hall, née Bankes, who has written books about the family including *Dorset Heritage*, states that he was 'unusually handsome and was possessed of personal magnetism that captivated men and women alike, whether in the London salons or the deserts of Arabia'. The Barbara Cartland figure that this conjures up – one of her heroes I mean – must after all these years be little more than an agreeably pious fancy.

The sad thing is that in his later years and especially after the death of Byron his persona caught up with him. The heavy drinking became real; the outrageous behaviour turned to genuine loutishness. In 1841 he was committed for trial on a charge of homosexuality. This would not of course be a sign of decadence in itself, but the point was that it had already happened to him once, in 1833, and he had been acquitted. To be tried for homosexuality once may be regarded as a misfortune; to be tried for it twice looks like carelessness; or rather it looks like an unhappy disregard for one's own welfare.

In any case it is doubtful if he really was gay. At the first trial public figures who could not afford to perjure themselves, like the Duke of Wellington and the headmaster of Harrow, had sworn that he was not. An assumption of sexual irregularity was part of the Romantic image; Byron was probably not incestuous either.

The exile that both Byron and Shelley had courted and won was vouchsafed to William Bankes too. Before this second trial could take place, he jumped bail and went to live abroad. He died in Venice fourteen years later and no doubt there were many British worthies who trusted it was a lesson he would profit by. But in these fourteen years he continued to send back to Kingston Lacy art treasures of every kind. His brother George had to pay for them but as William had made over his property to him before leaving England it cannot have been too much of a grievance.

William Bankes's method of acquiring these art treasures had always been that of an amateur. He frequently relied on the opinion of another amateur, his friend Byron, who is known to have advised him to buy *The Judgement of Solomon*. It seems not to have occurred to Bankes to go into the attribution. It would not have been difficult for him to find out that the seventeenth-century art historian Ridolfi who had declared the painting to be by Giorgione had ascribed more paintings to the young man than one could reasonably expect of a painter who had lived to be very old and had remained prolific to the end.

His method, if any of the romantic stories are to be believed, was also that of a pirate. Though not a soldier he was a kind of upper-class camp follower – he was with the Duke of Wellington in the Peninsular War – and as such took the opportunity to indulge not only in direct looting but in robbing the dead who had already looted. And even in the last years of his life he was exploiting such states of public misery as sieges, as he openly acknowledged in a letter from Venice: 'It was the accident of my being here during all the Siege that enabled me to pick up all these fine things. Since nobody had a farthing, anything might be had for money.'

William Bankes's piracy has a permanent memorial in the grounds as well as inside the house: a twenty-foot obelisk on a five-foot pedestal which he 'caused to be removed', according to the delicately worded inscription, from the island of Philae in 1819. It is raised even higher by a stone platform which he caused to be removed from the ruins of Hierassycaminon in Nubia. Dreadful as it is to think of all the straining and heaving and crushing involved in its transport the stone group gives an impression of serenity and triumph.

Triumphant it may well look. As the inscription explains, the obelisk and pedestal were dedicated 'to King Ptolemy Euergetes II and two Cleopatras his queens who authorised the priest of Isis in the isle of Philae to erect them about 150 years BC as a perpetual memorial of exemption from taxation'. It is not quite clear *who* was exempted from taxation but it was a good reason for erecting an obelisk.

The grounds of Kingston Lacy are at the time of writing a creative mess. Misinterpreting a placard at the main gate that said 'Whites only' we entered and got bogged down. The mud suggests a battlefield, and an army of cranes, grabs and diggers is drawn up and manoeuvring. But it is so delightful to see the house unwrapped again and one has so much confidence in the purpose and skill of the manoeuvring that it is a cheerful scene.

It is easy to perceive the former and future pleasantness of this very English park, of the sort that has been imitated all over Europe: flattish with no rocks or gorges or torrents or anything in particular but fine clumps and rows of trees, and rich grass. Away from the building site a magnificent herd of Red Devon cattle wanders heavily about like buffaloes. After so many fields all over Wessex full of black-and-white Friesians, it is a stirring sight that brings back a Devon childhood when all cows were red. The Devons always lead the Grand Parade at the Devon County Show, and the Supreme Champion is so often a Devon that people make jokes about nepotism.

By many tourists the complex of Corfe Castle and its village will be seen as the gem of the Bankes legacy. Their setting is certainly theatrical. A ridge of chalk pokes up through the usual Dorset chaos of soils and runs in a crescent right across Purbeck from the sea coast south of East Lulworth to end in Ballard Down at the north curve of Swanage Bay. The range is about 500 feet high and is unbroken except for a narrow gap in which rises a separate hill of comparable height. On it stands Corfe Castle.

The village lies in its shelter and in a modern sense is still under its patronage. It grew up along two roads, East Street and West Street, so called not because of the direction they take but because they lie to east and west of the town. West Street used to be the main street and was the centre of all the artistic and commercial activities involved in the preparation of the Purbeck stone that came from the quarries to the south. In the middle ages the Corfe stone trade had great prestige in England and in Europe. Men called de Corfe worked on Westminster Abbey and on churches abroad. Quantities of stone, both worked and unworked, were dragged north across the heath, along tracks which can still be seen, to be exported from the quaysides of Ower and other towns around Poole Harbour.

The life began to go out of the Purbeck stone industry in the seventeenth century and West Street is now quiet. East Street, on

Corfe Castle, from the north-east

the other hand, is exceedingly noisy, for it is part of the main road from Swanage to Wareham. Traffic comes rasping through, rushing at the gap in the chalk wall which leads to the world beyond Purbeck. There will certainly be a by-pass before long; it is a question of deciding on the route. There are six possibilities at present. The National Trust's choice is a road to the east of the town which could tunnel through the ridge.

Ralph Wightman suggests that the village of Corfe may be the 'least changed inhabited place in the county'. Houses continued to be built in stone long after the decline of the industry, so although experts say the standard of craftsmanship got perceptibly lower as the years went by there is nevertheless a feeling of homogeneity. One impression is that the pretty houses are simply too small for twentieth-century men and women. Any person of reasonable height would be doomed either to perpetual crouching or to permanent concussion.

People today are so accustomed to seeing churches and indeed cathedrals, which were built to be the largest objects in sight, dwarfed by tower blocks and power stations, that it is no visual surprise to find the church of Corfe overwhelmed by its castle. In any case they belong to the same species and look no more discrepant than a small toy next to a big toy.

Corfe Castle was built soon after the Norman Conquest on the site of a Saxon building which was either a palace or a hunting lodge. It was certainly royal as we know from the story of the murder of young King Edward in 978 by his stepmother Queen Elfrida, who was more ready than her own son Ethelred when it came to foul play. It is a most unpleasant tale, involving the betrayal of affection and some instances of unusually barefaced hypocrisy. There are several versions, each leaving a worse taste in the mouth than the last. A few years later Edward was canonised and the story took on further accretions: rays of celestial light, gushes of healing water, and a horse that would not carry the murderess in the funeral procession.

In 1572 the castle ceased to be royal. Elizabeth I sold it to Sir Christopher Hatton. In 1635 his widow sold it to Sir John Bankes, Attorney General, Chief Justice of the Common Pleas and owner of a considerable estate in Cumberland. He treated the castle as a family home and established his wife and children there before going off to serve his king. He was a whole-hearted Royalist, though like a good professional he got on quite well with the other side.

When the Civil War broke out the defence of the castle became the responsibility of Lady Bankes, always referred to in the storybooks of my childhood as Brave Dame Mary, a robust and admirable title by which I still think of her. Brave Dame Mary made a great success of her strange new duties. She prepared the castle to withstand a siege, and then held out for several years on and off, and finally through a long winter, organizing the practical matters of war and peace with total competence. Shakespeare, who was attracted to women who ran their castles well, would have liked her very much. In the end, she was defeated only by treachery.

She and her children – she was by this time a widow – were allowed to leave the castle in the early months of 1646 and almost immediately Parliament ordered that it should be put out of action. The deed was carried out with vindictive thoroughness. Far less damage than was done would have prevented it from becoming a politically viable fortress again. But it was blown to pieces.

Many of the pieces are still there, however: lopsided, misshapen, overgrown, out of place, but still there. There are many excellent maps and diagrams showing the layout of the castle as it was, but in fact there is enough left for one to experience, almost unaided, the space and purpose of the various parts of the castle; to walk from chamber to hall, from indoors to outdoors, through arches and gates, up stairs and steps, over dungeons where knights and pirates were imprisoned and into enclosed plots where a garden grew.

In spite of everything there is more left than there is of most old abbeys which had to contend only with wind and rain and not with gunpowder. And there is considerably more than survives of the other two castles known to have been built by the Normans in Dorset. There is no trace whatever of the one at Dorchester.

It is not difficult to imagine Corfe Castle as it once was, but it is anybody's guess what it would look like now if it had lived on for more than three centuries after the need for a real castle had gone for ever. After all, Sir John Bankes had begun to domesticate it even before the Civil War. Would Salvin, for example, have been hired in the nineteenth century to do what he did at Dunster?

Many writers have seen dignity and beauty in the death of a building when its time has come and its purpose has been served. I do not mean the elegiac feeling that a house has gradually and naturally turned into 'the accomplished past', as D. H. Lawrence said about Garsington Manor, nor the symbolic vision of Yeats

Erosion, Badbury Rings

when speaking about Coole Park, Lady Gregory's house: 'When she died the great house died too.' These are situations of peace and have little to do with Corfe Castle. In fact, Yeats's fine phrase has little to do with Coole Park either; the reality was that it could not be kept up, was sold to the Land Commission and finally demolished: a version of an all too common story.

More relevant to Corfe is what happened to Irish houses other than Coole Park, which escaped the Troubles. As Yeats, in another context, realised and as so many Irish and Anglo-Irish described, the Big House usually came to an end by the fires of war. Its passing was a direct result of revolutionary social and political change.

Sir Walter Scott has put it best of all. In *Waverley* Baron Bradwardine responds to the destruction of his mansion with these words:

> I did what I thought my duty and questionless they are doing what
> they think theirs. It grieves me sometimes to look upon these
> blackened walls of the house of my ancestors . . . But houses and
> families and men have a' stood lang eneuch when they have stood
> till they fall with honour.

Brave Dame Mary might well have uttered these noble words, especially the last sentence, as long, that is, as she was being true to the spirit rather than the letter of her situation. For the happy fact is that though she and her family did indeed stand with honour they did not fall, or at least not far.

At about the time that Sir John Bankes bought Corfe Castle he also bought the manor of Kingston Lacy, which after the destruction of the Castle was the obvious place for the family to settle. The heir, Sir Ralph, inherited his father's abilities, and Mary Bankes lived to see not only the Restoration but the foundations of the new house and all the signs of future prosperity.

The Bankes Estate is much more scattered than the Holnicote Estate which is a coherent whole. Corfe Castle is miles from Kingston Lacy with a great deal of land and property belonging to other people in between. The nearest tourist attraction to Kingston Lacy House is Badbury Rings. This site is best described as an Iron Age hill-fort, though it may have a much earlier history. Every guide-book stresses that it is as yet unexcavated. There are obviously revelations in store. There may well be evidence of a desperate battle with the Second Legion: the skeleton of a Briton, say, with a

Studland Heath and Bay

Nine Barrow Down

Roman spear embedded in his vertebrae. In the meantime, without evidence, we certainly come into contact again with the Durotriges, whose sad brave path to extinction we followed in West Dorset.

Anybody thinking that one Iron Age hill-fort is much like another would be shaken up in Dorset. Some of the differences are not of course basic: the beautiful profusion of mountain ash at Lambert's Castle, for example, or the eighteenth-century clump of trees in the very centre of Badbury Rings where all the habitation would have been. But compared with that of the other hill-forts the position of Badbury Rings does call for comment. It is so low. It commands a wide view certainly but at much its own level, whereas Eggardon Hill to the west dominates the entire landscape; it is perhaps the only place in Dorset which makes Golden Cap look like a detail in the coastline.

To speak of a year in the life of the settlement at Badbury, which by now is probably in its fifth millennium, may seem affected, but the last twelve months really have made a difference. When I visited the fort a year ago the three rings were criss-crossed and scarred with white erosion marks where the chalk had been exposed: visually interesting but not what either nature or man intended. Aerial photographs I have seen since then have shown these blemishes very clearly. But now the scene has changed. As Kingston Lacy House emerges from its restraints Badbury has been fenced in, temporarily. The grass is already growing over the scars, and a neat, sympathetic little path has been constructed to guide the visitors up to and around the tops of the ramparts and head them off the slopes. It will be a wonderful walk.

Some parts of the Bankes Estate are even more detached from Kingston Lacy than Corfe Castle is, for example Studland and its bay and heath. The road goes off to the left just before you enter Corfe village and runs along the chalk ridge to the north until, with Godlingston Heath to the north and Ballard Down to the south, it reaches the sea. Writers have pointed out how the Studland peninsula has always been protected against traffic from the east by the fact that there are only two ways to get to it: going right round Poole Harbour by road or crossing by water from Sandbanks. This deterrent applies today, they say, for the road is crowded and devious and the ferry is slow. With regard to the ferry they were lucky; on the day we were there it was not running at all.

Yet we were really the lucky ones. I shall never forget that evening on Studland, a November evening with nobody about. We

Fenced Dunes, Studland Bay

Car parks, Studland Bay

Old Harry

had driven downhill from the village of Studland, and on to the low level peninsula, past the closed booking-office and right along the approach to the ferry. It was beginning to get dark and the lights of Poole and Bournemouth were already on, suggesting merriment and bustle on the other side of the water but inspiring us with no wish whatever to be there; on the contrary.

I have known Hardy country all my life, but without ever feeling that it was helping me to understand him or his work better than attentive reading could do. This particular evening was different. As I looked across Poole Harbour from Brand's Bay, with the island of Brownsea dark and slumped and silent on my right, the western sky bore the direct and distinctive marks of the President of the Immortals. It was black and red with no subtler colour at all. It was capricious, cruel and impossible to reason with.

The way back to the village was across true Hardy heath, never seen now in other parts of Dorset; neither imagination nor the eye of faith fuelled by wide reading can conjure it up. It is a secret world, inhabited by invisible birds crying in every tone of knowledge and ignorance, lament and triumph; a dark brown and purple land, wild and wet and bleak, bare although so much is growing there.

To the left of the road lies Studland Beach and here in the growing darkness reigns the Spinner of the Years. Through the centuries he has said 'Now' to events as dire as the meeting of the *Titanic* and the iceberg. What has happened in nature is no doubt his doing too: the sea's drawing back from the land; it used to come up as far as the west bank of Little Sea which still gleams at night in harmony with the real sea though it is salt no longer. But this shaping of the land was so gradual as to seem peaceful, and indeed did no harm to anybody.

The Spinner's name is a euphemism, however, and what has happened on Studland Beach to humans is more in keeping with his characteristic violence. Pirates who had been imprisoned in Corfe Castle at the time of its many-sided heyday were dragged here from their dungeons and hanged. The D-Day invasion was rehearsed here, and the whole peninsula shook with the bombardment. One fears for the future. The Spinner of the Years has struck oil in Studland, and now there is a real threat to man and bird and beast, and to the land itself. One comfort is that the Spinner will have to take on the whole of the National Trust.

The way home from Studland to Devon is through Wareham so we had to pass Corfe Castle again. As we were by then heading west there was still a little light behind it. Many of the more scattered stones are overgrown, and in broad daylight, though Corfe is still indomitably the work of man, they look like rocks on a tor. That evening, perhaps every evening at sunset, the whole castle had turned into a craggy hill.

At the entrance to Badbury Rings during the 1970s there was a notice which stated that the public had no access to the site as of right but only by permission of Mr Henry John Ralph Bankes, the owner. Already, had the public but known it, the situation was changing. Quite early in the decade Mr Bankes had invited two men to an interview, sworn them to secrecy, and then uttered the magic words that, through the ages, all great landowners with proper respect for their estates must have been proud to speak: 'One day all this will be yours.' The two men were representatives of the National Trust.

AVON

(formerly Bristol and parts of Gloucestershire and Somerset)
1684½ acres owned, 322½ acres protected

BATH

Assembly Rooms Built in 1771 by John Wood the younger. An important addition to Bath at its most fashionable period. Frequently mentioned in the works of Jane Austen and in Charles Dickens's *Pickwick Papers*. Let to the City Council whose important Museum of Costume is displayed in the basement.

Bushey Norwood ½m N of Rainbow Wood Farm, between Claverton Manor and the golf course, 66 acres of farmland (on which is the site of a field system and of a walled courtyard with a hearth) crossed by a public right of way (footpath). The property is bounded on the north by the rampart of Bathampton hill-fort.

Rainbow Wood Farm On Claverton Down, 1m SE of Bath. There are Iron Age field enclosures. Access limited to public footpaths.

BRISTOL

Blaise Hamlet 4m N of central Bristol, W of Henbury village, just N of B4057. 1¾ acres. A group of ten cottages of differing design, irregularly disposed round a green. Built in Picturesque style in 1809 by John Nash for John Harford to house the Blaise estate pensioners. Cottages not open.

Frenchay Moor 5m NE of central Bristol, 2m S of Winterbourne on B4427. 8 acres. Managed by Winterbourne Parish Council.

Leigh Woods On left bank of the Avon, by Clifton Suspension Bridge, NE of A369. 159½ acres of woodland, including Nightingale Valley and the Iron Age promontory fort of Stokeleigh.

Shirehampton Park 4m NW of central Bristol, astride the Avonmouth road (A4). 99 acres overlooking the Avon. Part is used as a golf course.

Westbury College In College Road, Westbury-on-Trym, 3m N of the centre of Bristol. The fifteenth-century gatehouse of the College of Priests (founded in the thirteenth century) of which John Wycliff was a prebend.

CADBURY CAMP 2½m E of Clevedon
39½ acres on which is an Iron Age hill-fort.

CLEVEDON COURT 1½m E of Clevedon, on the Bristol road
14½ acres. A manor house, once fortified, with additions made in every century since the thirteenth. Fourteenth-century chapel, eighteenth-century terraced garden.

DOLEBURY WARREN, CHURCHILL 12m SE of Bristol, E of A38 above Churchill
225 acres. The wild and barren hill top forms one of the finest viewpoints in the Mendips. Dominated by an impressive Iron Age fort, the remains of a Celtic field system and the medieval pillow mounds of the rabbit warren are visible; also evidence of lead and other minerals. The unusual combination of heather moorland and limestone grassland makes the Warren a site of particular interest. Managed by the Avon Wildlife Trust. Bought in 1983 with grants from the Countryside Commission, the Directorate of Ancient Monuments and the Mendip Trust, and money bequeathed by Mr F. L. Sharp. Access by public footpath starting from A38, ½m S of junction with A368. Roadside parking only.

DYRHAM PARK 7m N of Bath, 12m E of Bristol; approached from the Bath–Stroud road
274 acres. The house was built 1692–1702 by William Blathwayt, Secretary of State and Secretary at War, on the site of the earlier house of his wife's family, the Wynters. The east front is an unaltered design by William Talman, but the west front is a few years earlier and documents show it to have been the work of a little-known Huguenot, S. Hauduroy. The panelling, tapestries and furniture in the late seventeenth-century rooms reflect the Dutch taste of the period as do the pictures, leather wall-hangings and Delft tulip-holders. The state bed with its original satins and velvets, part of a royal suite of c.1705, has been returned to the house on long loan from the Lady Lever Art Gallery. One of the country's oldest herds of fallow deer graze the park.

FAILAND 4m W of central Bristol, on S side of A369, E of Lower Failand overlooking the Severn
363 acres, including several farms and woodlands.

HORTON COURT 3m NE of Chipping Sodbury, ¾m N of Horton, 1m W of the Bath–Stroud road
A Cotswold manor house, restored and somewhat altered in the nineteenth century, but containing a twelfth-century Norman hall and early Renaissance features, with 146 acres of farmland. The garden has an unusual late Perpendicular ambulatory detached from the house.

LITTLE SOLSBURY HILL Between Swainswick (A46) and Batheaston (A4), 2½m NE of Bath
22½ acres of flat hilltop (625ft) with a fine Iron Age hill-fort, the ramparts faced with dry-stone walling. Excavated by the University of Bristol Spelaeological Society; finds in its museum. Views over the Avon valley, Bath and four counties.

MIDDLE HOPE (WOODSPRING) 5m N of Weston-super-Mare
158 acres stretching over 2m of coast with views across the Bristol Channel to the Welsh Mountains and across the Somerset Marshes to the Mendips. Bought in 1968 with Enterprise Neptune funds. Access from Sand Bay to

most of this land. There is a complex of low banks and foundations at St Thomas's Head and a possible barrow group at Middle Hope.

MONK'S STEPS, KEWSTOKE On N edge of Weston-super-Mare
The Monk's (or St Kew's) Steps and 2½ acres. Views over the Severn Estuary and towards Bristol.

REDCLIFFE BAY
A coastal belt of 2 acres, about 200yd long, which is crossed by the mariners' footpath from Clevedon to Portishead.

SAND POINT, KEWSTOKE 5m N of Weston-super-Mare
32 acres of coastal headland adjoining the Trust's Middle Hope property. 'Castle Batch' is probably a Norman motte and the low mound to the east a round barrow.

DORSET

20,240 acres owned, 961½ acres protected

BELLE VUE FARM On Isle of Purbeck, about 2m SW of Swanage
51 acres of rough grazing above the cliffs. Access by public footpaths, including a stretch of the South-West Coastal Footpath.

BROWNSEA ISLAND In Poole harbour about 1½m SSE of Poole near Sandbanks
500 acres. The island is heath and woodland. Magnificent views of the Dorset coast, miles of woodland path and open glades and a mile of beach for bathing. 200-acre Nature Reserve managed by the Dorset Naturalists' Trust with access for guided parties at fixed times, containing a heronry, a marsh and two lakes which are sanctuaries for wildfowl. Camping for Scouts and Guides only through their respective Associations.

BURTON CLIFF, BURTON BRADSTOCK
83½ acres. A high bluff of cliff running west from Burton Bradstock village rising to 100ft sheer above the sea before dropping down to Freshwater Bay. Inland it slopes to the encircling arm of the River Bride. There are both riverside and cliff walks, access being unrestricted along the clifftop and river bank. Includes a stretch of the South-West Coastal Footpath.

THE CERNE GIANT On Giant Hill (600ft), N of Cerne Abbas, 8m N of Dorchester, just E of A352
A Romano-British figure of a man, 180ft high, brandishing a 120ft club, cut in the chalk.

CLOUDS HILL 9m E of Dorchester, 1½m E of Waddock crossroads (B3390). 1m N of Bovington Camp
A cottage with 7½ acres, to which T. E. Lawrence (Lawrence of Arabia) retired on leaving the RAF.

CONEY'S CASTLE
86 acres adjacent to Lambert's Castle. A hilltop and surrounding land partly covered by scrub, gorse and bracken. Fine views over the Marshwood Vale. The site of an Iron Age hill-fort. Access on foot to the hilltop.

CORFE CASTLE ESTATE 5m NW of Swanage and 4m SE of Wareham on A351
Corfe Castle, an important medieval royal fortification commanding a cleft in the Purbeck Hills, was acquired by the Bankes family in 1635 when bought by Sir John, Attorney-General to Charles I. His wife, Lady Bankes, withstood two long sieges in the Civil War, only surrendering to the Parliamentary forces after treachery in 1646, after which the Castle was slighted. Today its ruins are a dramatic focus for a 7294 acre estate comprising 50 cottages in the village of Corfe Castle, Corfe Common, Purbeck stone quarries and coast at Seacombe near Langton Matravers, the Nature Reserves (3,581 acres) of Middlebere, Studland and Godlingston Heaths, farmland (2,800 acres), 254 acres of amenity woodland, 4 miles of beach at Studland, including Shell Bay, Studland Bay and Old Harry Rocks.

CREECH: GRANGE ARCH 3m W of Corfe Castle, 4m E of Worbarrow Bay; commonly called Bond's Folly
In the Purbeck Hills, silhouetted against the sky, south of Creech Grange. Built early in the eighteenth century by Denis Bond of Creech Grange.

CROOK HILL, BEAMINSTER
6 acres. A fine viewpoint near Winyard's Gap.

EGGARDON HILL
47 acres of unimproved downland, including half of the land covered by the Iron Age fort; fine views over Marshwood Vale and the sea.

FONTMELL DOWN Between Shaftesbury and Blandford
149 acres. A superb ridge of unimproved downland, important botanically and archaeologically with Iron Age cross dykes. Fine views over the Blackmore Vale: Thomas Hardy's Dorset. Access by public footpaths; no car parking facilities.

Fontmell Down: Gourd's Farm, East Compton 132½ acres of downland next to the Trust's Fontmell Down property

GOLDEN CAP ESTATE
1974 acres of hill, cliff, farmland, undercliff and beach including about 5m of the coast between Charmouth and Eypemouth and grazing rights over 35 acres. The estate is served by 15m of footpath, including one through route along the coast of 6m. Access by car to viewpoints on Stonebarrow Hill and Chardown. By car to the sea only at Charmouth, Seatown and Eypemouth. On foot, from Morcombelake, there is access to the beach at St Gabriel's. There is access to a very large part of the estate, but visitors are especially asked not to damage crops or disturb stock and to remember that the preservation of the wildlife of animals and plants is of particular importance.

Black Venn 49 acres, including 29 acres of cliff leased to the Dorset Naturalists' Trust.

Cain's Folly 31 acres of undercliff and rough pasture at Charmouth. Includes a stretch of the South-West Coastal Footpath.

Chardown Hill & Upcot Farm Access by car from A35 at Morcombelake to picnic places on hilltop. Views of the coast and inland over the Marshwood Vale to Lambert's Castle and Pilsdon Pen.

Chardown, Stonebarrow & the Undercliffs Managed in consultation with the Dorset Naturalists' Trust for the conservation of wildlife.

Doghouse Hill 54 acres including twin hills immediately west of Thornecombe Beacon and spectacular 300ft high cliffs.

Downhouse Farm 176 acres with grazing rights over Eype Down (35 acres), ¾m of undercliff and farmland reaching from Eypemouth to Thornecombe Beacon (508ft), where there is a group of three barrows, of which the Trust owns two.

Filcombe & Norchard Farms 252 acres of farmland and woods.

Golden Cap 26 acres of the summit (618ft) of the highest cliffs in the south of England. A memorial to Lord Antrim, of Purbeck stone, was set up in 1978 on the top of the cliff beside the coastal footpath.

Hardown Hill 25 acres. Part of the manor of Berne and Morcombelake, the land occupies much of the crest and slopes of this flat-topped hill with views north over the Marshwood Vale and south past Golden Cap to the sea. It is open to the public on foot at all times from Morcombelake.

Ridge Cliff & West Cliff, Seatown 170 acres of cliff, undercliff and farmland on each side of Seatown.

The Saddle 8 acres forming a col between Golden Cap and Langdon Hill.

St Gabriel's 192 acres of undercliff and clifftop with steep access to sea reached only on foot from Morcombelake. Ruins of thirteenth-century chapel.

Shedbush Farm 61 acre grassland farm.

Ship Farm 39 acre grassland farm.

The Spittles 126 acres, including 94 acres of cliff, leased to the Dorset Naturalists' Trust as a nature reserve. Includes part of the South-West Coastal Footpath.

Stonebarrow Hill & Westhay Farm 335 acres. 274 acres of farm, undercliff and hill, 1½ acres of enclosed heathland, formerly a Ministry of Defence Radar Station. The building has been converted as an information point and as accommodation for working parties. Access by car to the hill from A35 at Charmouth; car parking; extensive public access for picnicking and walking; bridleways.

HARDY MONUMENT 6m SW of Dorchester, on the Martinstown-Portisham road
¾ acre. Erected in 1846 to Vice-Admiral Sir Thomas Masterman Hardy, flag-captain of *Victory* at Trafalgar. Views over Weymouth Bay.

HARDY'S COTTAGE, HIGHER BOCKHAMPTON 3m NE of Dorchester, ½m S of A35.
A small thatched house, the birthplace of Thomas Hardy in 1840. Garden of 1 acre. There is a small collection of items of interest connected with Hardy.

KINGSTON LACY ESTATE 2m NW of Wimborne on W side of B3082
The home of the Bankes family for over three hundred years: the original brick house was designed for Sir Ralph Bankes, son of Sir John the Attorney General to Charles I, in 1663–5 by Sir Roger Pratt. It was later altered and encased in stone by Sir Charles Barry for W. J. Bankes, the traveller and collector of the family, in 1835–9. The superb collection of paintings includes works by Titian, Rubens and Velasquez and two series of family portraits by van Dyck and Lely. W. J. Bankes's interest in Egypt is reflected both within the house and in the obelisk from the Island of Philae re-erected in the grounds. The house is set in 13 acres of formal gardens and woodland walks surrounded by a park of 254 acres which supports a herd of Red Devon cattle. To the NE of the park lies Badbury Rings, an Iron-Age fort with Bronze Age burial mounds. The estate of some 8795 acres includes 14 farms and parts of the villages of Shapwick and Pamphill, and the proposed National Nature Reserve of Holt Heath (1216 acres).

LAMBERT'S CASTLE HILL 4½m E of Axminster of the S side of B3165
167 acres. Hilltop (842ft) and surrounding land, covered with gorse and bracken, and a belt of wild woodland on the north escarpment – the site of an Iron Age hill-fort and with a round barrow. Wide views to Chesil Bank on the east and to Dartmoor on the west.

LEWESDON HILL 3m W of Beaminster, 1m S of Broadwinsor, ¼m W of B3162
27 acres of the wooded summit (894ft). Views over Devon, Dorset, Somerset and the sea.

PILSDON PEN 3m SW of Broadwindsor on B3164
One of Dorset's landmarks, dominated by an Iron Age hill-fort, 905ft. 36 acres of rough grazing, approached by footpath off B3164, at the foot of Cockpit Hill.

RINGMOOR: TURNWORTH DOWN
134 acres of unimproved downland, the site of a remarkably preserved Romano-British settlement surrounded by old deciduous woodland. Fine views from the Down. Car parking at the Okeford Hill picnic site, owned by Dorset County Council. Approach on foot along the Ridgeway from Okeford Hill; a public footpath crosses the property.

SOUTHDOWN FARM 7m SE of Dorchester, in Ringstead Bay; access 5m from Weymouth along A353 at the Upton turning past Ringstead RAF camp
273 acres of farmland, with a sea front of 700yds. Views over Weymouth Bay and Portland Bill. Cars may be brought to the crest of the Down only and access to the sea is on foot (½m).

Burning Cliff & Whitenothe Cliff 107 acres of cliffs adjoining Southdown Farm, between Burning Cliff and Whitenothe. Undercliff formed by landslips over the gault clay with great cliffs of chalk and greensand behind, which isolate the area from the hinterland. The Burning Cliff is said to be

so called from peat fires which burned for six years. Whitenothe cliff path is too dangerous for walkers; it is the legendary smugglers' escape route chronicled in *Moonfleet* by J. Meade Falkner.

TOLPUDDLE: MARTYRS' MEMORIAL 7m NE of Dorchester, on S side of A35
A seat commemorates the labourers condemned to transportation in 1834.

WEST BEXINGTON
Lime Kiln Hill 37 acres. 17 acres of former stone workings and rough grazing on the crest of the ridge which overlooks the Chesil Bank to the south and the Bride Valley to the north. 20 acres of rough grazing and farmland adjoining the Trust's Lime Kiln property.

WHITECLIFF FARM & BALLARD DOWN On Isle of Purbeck
222 acres. 108 acres of downland, steep slopes and undercliff with fine views of the Dorset coast and good footpaths. Also 114 acres of undulating farmland. Access by public footpaths and a bridleway across the down, with the coastal footpath along the cliff edge.

WINYARD'S GAP Above Chedington. 4m SE of Crewkerne, on S side of A356
16 acres of woodland, given in 1949 as a memorial to the men of the 43rd (Wessex) Division who fell in the 1939–45 war.

SOMERSET

(*see also* Avon)
16,830½ acres owned, *26 acres protected*

BARRINGTON COURT 3m NE of Ilminster, at E end of Barrington, ½m E of B3168
219 acres. The house was built in the mid-sixteenth century by Lord Daubeny and is externally little altered. It has late Gothic windows and twisted finials. The stable block, now a dwelling, is red brick dating from 1670.

BLACKDOWN HILLS 2m S of Wellington (A38), ½m E of the Wellington-Hemyock road
61 acres. Views over the Vale of Taunton to Exmoor and the Quantocks and – on a clear day – across the Bristol Channel to the Welsh mountains.

Wellington Monument ½m W of above property. An obelisk, built in 1817–18 to commemorate the exploits of the Duke of Wellington. The architect was T. Lee.

BREAN DOWN 2m SW of Weston-super-Mare, the S arm of Weston Bay.
159 acres. A bold headland 300ft high. There is a small Iron Age promontory fort, field systems and evidence of occupation from Beaker times onwards.

BRENT KNOLL 3m E of Burnham-on-Sea, 1m N of Exit 22 on M5.
A prominent hill (450ft) in the Somerset Levels, dominated by an Iron Age hill-fort. 33 acres, including the summit, woodlands on the northern slopes and two meadows. No car park. Footpaths to the summit from Brent Knoll and East Brent villages. Village roads unsuitable for parking.

BROOMFIELD HILL 6m N of Taunton
110 acres acquired in 1972

BRUTON DOVECOTE ½m S of Bruton across railway, ¼m W of B3081
A sixteenth-century roofless dovecote.

CHEDDAR CLIFFS 8m NW of Wells
375 acres, including 107 acres on the north side of the famous gorge (B3135), at its lower end, with the Lion and Monkey Rocks. From Sun Hole Cave have come Upper Palaeolithic artefacts, also evidence of Neolithic and Beaker occupation. Much of the land is of special scientific

interest and part is managed by the Somerset Trust for Nature Conservation as a nature reserve with limited access. Roadside parking at Black Rock Gate on B3135 at SW corner of property; public footpath.

COLERIDGE COTTAGE At W end of Nether Stowey, on S side of A39, 8m W of Bridgwater

Here S. T. Coleridge lived, 1797–1800, and wrote *The Ancient Mariner* and the first part of *Christabel*.

DUNSTER CASTLE 3m SE of Minehead, E of Dunster village, on S side of A39

Fortified home of the Luttrells for 600 years: the Castle and its park are dramatically set between the wooded hills of Exmoor and the sea, where mild winters encourage semi-tropical shrubs on the terraced walks. The mansion was remodelled by Anthony Salvin in the nineteenth century; the fine seventeenth-century staircase and plasterwork were retained. Cromwellian stables.

Grabbist Hill 1m W of Dunster Village. 55 acres of open space with steeply wooded oak hillside. Magnificent views over Dunster Castle to the Quantocks and Exmoor. Access by public footpaths and bridle ways.

EBBOR GORGE 3m NW of Wells

142 acres of wooded limestone gorge in the Mendip Hills, leased to the Nature Conservancy Council, which manages it as a nature reserve, with public access over footpaths. There are caves and rock shelters which have yielded material ranging from Upper Palaeolithic to Romano-British. A memorial stone to Sir Winston Churchill was unveiled by Mrs Piers Dixon, Sir Winston Churchill's grand-daughter, on 17 May 1967.

EXMOOR

Holnicote Estate, Dunkery etc. E & S of Porlock, astride A39, extending 6m S from N coast. 12,443 acres, including 6270 acres of the Moor, Dunkery and Selworthy Beacons (from which there are views over the Bristol Channel), Bossington Hill, 4m of coast, fifteen farms and most of the villages of Allerford, Bossington, Selworthy, Tivington, Luccombe and the hamlets of West Luccombe, Brandish Street, Horner and Lynch, with many typical examples of local cottage architecture. There are ancient pack-horse bridges at Horner, West Luccombe and Allerford, and groups of round barrows, a stone circle and the hill-fort of Bury Castle. Holnicote House, which is not of architectural importance, is let to the Holiday Fellowship.

South Hill, Dulverton 93 acres of moorland adjoining Winsford Hill.

Winsford Hill Between Exford (B3223) and Dulverton (B3222) 1288 acres of moorland, on which is the Bronze Age barrow group known as Wambarrows and also the Caratacus Stone.

GLASTONBURY 4 acres of land at Wellhouse Lane.

GLASTONBURY TOR A conical hill E of Glastonbury on N side of A361, with views over and beyond the Vale of Avalon

62½ acres, including Tor Field, adjoining fields and a strip of orchard. At the summit (525ft) an excavation by Mr P. A. Rahtz has recovered the plans of two superimposed churches of St Michael, of which only the fifteenth-century tower remains; this is held as a memorial to Dr Jex-Blake, Dean of Wells from 1891 to 1915. Lower on the Tor are undisturbed buildings, probably monastic.

KING JOHN'S HUNTING LODGE, AXBRIDGE

Stands prominently on the corner of the Square. It was built about 1500 and illustrates the new-found prosperity of the merchant class at the time. On lease to Sedgemoor D C as a museum.

LYTES CARY On W side of the Fosse Way (A37), 2½m NE of Ilchester, 2½m SE of Somerton; turn W off the Fosse Way along A372 towards Langport for 400yd, then N towards Charlton Adam; house ½m up on E side

365 acres. A typical Somerset manor house. The chapel is of the fourteenth century, the great hall of the fifteenth; additions in later centuries. The home for 500 years of the Lyte family. Here was the garden upon which Sir Henry Lyte based his *Niewe Herball*, published in 1578, the most important horticultural work of that time.

MARTOCK: THE TREASURER'S HOUSE 1m NW of A303 between Ilminster and Ilchester

A small house dating from the thirteenth and fourteenth centuries, once lived in by the Treasurer of Wells Cathedral. Contains a fine medieval hall, built by 1293, and kitchen. Access to the great hall and kitchen.

MONTACUTE 4m W of Yeovil, on N side of A3088

303 acres. The house was built in the last decade of the sixteenth century by Sir Edward Phelips, Speaker of the House of Commons and Master of the Rolls under James I. It has an H-shaped ground plan and is built of Ham Hill stone. Its external features include oriel windows, curvilinear and finialled gables, open balustraded parapets, carved statues of the Nine Worthies standing in niches on the east front and fluted angle columns. Fine heraldic glass, plasterwork and panelling. Some fine tapestries, English portraits and furniture – a bequest from Sir Malcolm Stewart Bt. The National Portrait Gallery exhibits sixteenth-century portraits in the Long Gallery. The contemporary garden was restored by Mrs Ellen Phelips and her gardener Mr Pridham in the middle of the nineteenth century, and the present layout dates largely from this time. The two Elizabethan garden pavilions in the east forecourt are among the best garden features of the period and originally flanked the entrance front. The property, which includes twenty-four cottages in the village and 303 acres, takes its name from the Mons Acutus (St Michael's Hill).

MUCHELNEY: PRIEST'S HOUSE 1½m S of Langport.

Late medieval house with large Gothic hall window, originally the residence of the secular priests who served the parish church. Repaired under the supervision of the Society for the Protection of Ancient Buildings.

THE QUANTOCKS

Beacon Hill & Bicknoller Hill 2½m E of Williton, 6m W of Holford off A39. 626½ acres of moorland, including the Iron Age fort of Trendle Ring (AM). Magnificent views over the Bristol Channel, the Vale of Taunton Deane and to Exmoor.

Holford Fields 3m W of Nether Stowey, on W side of the Minehead-Bridgwater road (A39). 27½ acres. 22½ acres of pastureland and orchard given by Mr. O. M. Dalton in 1932–35. Small pasture field of 5 acres. No public access.

Longstone Hill W of Holford. 61 acres of open moorland adjoining Willoughby Cleeve, with fine views.

Shervage Wood 2m W of Nether Stowey on S side of A39. 136 acres of oak woodland, oak coppice and moorland with views over the Bristol Channel.

Willoughby Cleeve ½m W of Holford near Alfoxton (Alfoxden) Park at the foot of the Quantocks. 77½ acres of woodland, agricultural land and moorland. No access to agricultural land.

SEDGEMOOR & ATHELNEY

Burrow Mump 2½m SW of Othery just S of A361. ·An isolated hill of 9¼ acres, with views in all directions. On the summit is an unfinished late eighteenth-century chapel built over the foundations of an earlier one. A small Norman castle had previously occupied the site.

Cock Hill About half-way between Bridgwater and Glastonbury, near Chilton Polden and Edington. ¾ acre on crest of the Polden Hills. The course of the Roman road from Ilchester to the mouth of the River Parrett, via the western part of the Polden Hills, bounds the property on the north.

Ivythorn & Walton Hills 1m S of Street, W of B3151. 88½ acres of highland and wood. Views. The course of the Romanized ridgeway on the eastern part of the Polden Hills runs through the length of both properties.

The Mill, High Ham 2m N of Langport, ½m E of High Ham. A thatched windmill dating from 1820 and in use until 1910.

Red Hill 1m NW of Curry Rivel (B3153), 3m W of Langport, on S edge of Sedgemoor. 2½ acres of hilltop, with views to Glastonbury Tor, the Quantocks and the Mendips.

Turn Hill 4m N of Langport, 1m W of High Ham. 1¼ acres, looking across the battlefield of Sedgemoor to the Quantocks.

STOKE-SUB-HAMDON PRIORY Just N of A3088, 2m W of Montacute, between Yeovil & Ilminster.
2 acres. Formerly the residence of the priests of the chantry of St Nicholas in the vanished Beauchamp manor house nearby. The farm buildings of Ham Hill stone date from the fourteenth and fifteenth centuries and the great hall and screens passage of the chantry house remain. Only the hall is open to visitors.

TINTINHULL HOUSE 5m NW of Yeovil, ½m S of A303, on E outskirts of Tintinhull
4 acres. A fine small house, *c.*1700, with a pediment and hipped roof. The beautiful formal garden was largely created by Mrs P. E. Reiss.

WELLS: TOR HILL Just E of the city, on N side of the Shepton Mallet road (A371).
19½ acres, with views of the cathedral and the surrounding country.

WEST PENNARD COURT BARN 3m E of Glastonbury, 7m S of Wells, 1½m S of West Pennard (A361).
A fifteenth-century barn of five bays, with a roof of interesting construction.

WILTSHIRE

6000½ acres owned, *409½ acres protected*

AVEBURY 6m W of Marlborough, 1m N of Bath road (A4) at the junction of A361 and B4003
912 acres. Perhaps the most important Megalithic ceremonial monument in Europe: about 1800 BC. The site of 27 acres, with circles of Sarsen stones, is enclosed by a bank and ditch and approached by an avenue of megaliths. The property includes 76 acres of Windmill Hill (1½m to the north-west), the Neolithic causewayed enclosure which has become the type-site for Neolithic A culture in Britain. It was excavated by Alexander Keiller, and the finds from Avebury and Windmill Hill are displayed in the museum situated north of the church. Under the guardianship of the Department of the Environment.

CHERHILL DOWN & OLDBURY CASTLE On A4, between Calne and Beckhampton
138½ acres of unimproved downland, including the Iron Age fort (but not the White Horse or the monument) approached by footpaths from the A4. Fine views from the ridge (852ft).

CLEY HILL 3m W of Warminster, on the Somerset border, on N side of A362
66 acres. A chalk hill 800ft high, on which is a univallate Iron Age hill-fort; within it two bowl-barrows.

DINTON 9m W of Salisbury, on the N side of B3089

Dinton Park, Philipps House & Hyde's House (*see* separate entry below) The property includes a farm, three cottages and the eastern rampart of Wick Ball Camp, an Iron Age hill-fort. 205½ acres. Philipps House, formerly a seat of the Wyndham family, was completed in 1816 by Jeffry Wyatt (later Sir Jeffry Wyattville), in the neo-Classical style. It is let as a holiday home to the Young Women's Christian Association. The 1st Baron Milford gave the furniture.

Hyde's House Close to the church. Built in the Wren manner, probably about 1725, and incorporates Tudor portions. It is let and not open.

Little Clarendon & Lawes Cottage ¼m E of Dinton Church. 29 acres. Little Clarendon is a stone Tudor house of the late fifteenth century. Lawes Cottage is a seventeenth-century stone building, once the home of William Lawes, the composer; it is let and not open. Given in 1940 by Mrs Engleheart, with a collection of furniture, other contents and an endowment, in memory of her husband. Little Clarendon open on written application to the tenant.

FIGSBURY RING 4m NE of Salisbury, ½m N of London road (A30)
27 acres with views over Salisbury. An Iron Age A hill-fort, enclosing 15 acres, univallate, with an inner quarry ditch and traces of an outer defence at the eastern entrance. Excavated in 1924 by Capt. & Mrs B. Howard Cunnington; finds in Devizes Museum.

GREAT CHALFIELD MANOR 3m NE of Bradford-on-Avon, via B3109
The moated house is an example of late Gothic domestic architecture, *c.* 1480. There is a great hall with screen and contemporary mural portrait of the builder. Restored by Mr Harold Brakspear, from drawings made by T. L. Walker, a pupil of Pugin, in the 1830s.

HOLT: THE COURTS 3m E of Bradford-on-Avon, 3m W of Melksham, entrance on S side of bridge following wall with overhanging beech
The Courts were where the weavers brought their disputes for arbitration until the end of the eighteenth century. The richly decorated façade dates from about 1700. The house is let and not open. The garden with its hedged vistas and fine trees is most attractive.

LACOCK ABBEY & VILLAGE 3m S of Chippenham, just E of A350
320 acres, including the abbey, most of the village, Manor Farm and Bewley Common. The abbey has thirteenth-century cloisters, sacristy, chapter house and nuns' parlour. After the Reformation, Sir William Sharington adapted the monastic remains to make a Tudor mansion. Its chief features are the octagonal tower overlooking the Avon, twisted chimney-stacks and large courtyard with half-timbered gables and clock-house. In 1753 Sanderson Miller made changes in the 'Gothick' taste; and the house saw further changes in 1828. Here Fox Talbot in 1835 invented the photographic process named after him. There are fine black walnut trees (*Juglans nigra*) in the approach to the abbey.

Lacock Village The cottages are of diverse architecture from the thirteenth to the nineteenth century, including a fourteenth-century house of cruck construction, a fourteenth-century tithe barn, the domed eighteenth-century lock-up and a sixteenth-century barn, now housing the Fox Talbot Photographic Museum.

LOCKERIDGE DENE 3m W of Marlborough, 1m S of the Bath road (A4)
12 acres of agricultural land in two plots, on which are examples of Sarsen stones, known locally as Grey Wethers.

PEPPERBOX HILL 5m SE of Salisbury, on N side of A36
72 acres of open down, with juniper bushes. Views. The Pepperbox is a seventeenth-century folly. Grimstead Beeches, two woods totalling 13 acres just north of the hill.

PIGGLE DENE 3m W of Marlborough, on N side of the Bath road (A4)
9 acres containing more Grey Wethers.

SALISBURY

Joiners' Hall in St Ann Street. Formerly the hall of a livery company. Only the timbered façade, dating from about 1550, is left. Let as an antique shop and not open.

Mompesson House On N side of Choristers' Green. One of the finest houses in the Close, built in 1701 by Charles Mompesson, MP for Old Sarum, with original panelling. Forty years later his brother-in-law, Charles Longueville, installed the sumptuous plasterwork ceilings and the fine staircase.

STONEHENGE DOWN 1–3m W of Amesbury, at junction of A303 & A360
1438 acres of farmland round Stonehenge, including the Fargo Plantation and Winterbourne Stoke Clump. Some of the finest barrows of the Early and Middle Bronze Age Wessex culture (finds in Devizes Museum). Other remains include the Cursus (late Neolithic, contemporary with the earliest phase of Stonehenge) and half the Avenue.

STOURHEAD At Stourton (B3092), 3m NW of Mere (A303)
2645 acres, including the pleasure grounds, the house with its contents, the village of Stourton, some 300 acres of woodland and King Alfred's

Tower. The house was designed in 1721 by Colen Campbell for Henry Hoare (the banker) whose son, Henry, laid out from 1741 the pleasure grounds with their lakes and temples, which are among the finest examples of eighteenth-century landscape design. The shores and lower woodlands contain some of the most magnificent specimens of conifers, tulip trees (*liriodendron*), beeches and rhododendrons in the country, and include many rarities. Beautiful throughout the year. Two wings to the house were added about 1800 by Sir Richard Colt Hoare. The house, which was partly burned in 1902, contains collections of works of art, notably furniture designed by Thomas Chippendale the younger. The estate includes the greater part of the Neolithic causewayed enclosure of White Sheet Down, a group of bowl-barrows and half the Iron Age hill-fort known as White Sheet Castle. In Park Hill Woods is a bivallate hill-fort, presumably Iron Age. The downland contains a rich variety of plants and several archaeological features closely linked with those on White Sheet Hill. Access via lane running east from B3092 at Red Lion Inn; parking at laneside.

WARMINSTER: BOREHAM FIELD
A 6 acre field with a right of way across it on the south side of the Warminster–Salisbury road.

WESTWOOD MANOR 1½m SW of Bradford-on-Avon, off B3109
59½ acres. A stone manor house of the late fifteenth century, altered in 1610, but retaining late Gothic and Jacobean windows and fine Jacobean plasterwork. Situated by the parish church. Modern topiary garden.

WHITE BARROW ¾m S of Tilshead, 7m NW of Stonehenge, ¼m W of A360
3 acres, with a Neolithic earthen long barrow with well-defined side ditches. Access by public footpath from main road.

WIN GREEN HILL 5m SE of Shaftesbury, ½m NE of B3081
38 acres, 911ft high. The highest point in Cranborne Chase, crowned by a tree circle. Views to the Quantocks and the Isle of Wight. The low bowl-barrow in the Clump was known as Beacon Barrow in the tenth century. The boundary includes about ¾m of the Ridgeway – where it is joined by the Ox Drove.

INDEX